From Harl...
JUDY CH...

Don't miss any of the...
of the Randall family.

THE RANDALLS: WYOMING WINTER
March 2002
a special volume containing the first two
Brides for Brothers books:
COWBOY CUPID & COWBOY DADDY

RANDALL RICHES
April 2002
Rich's story,
available from Harlequin American Romance

THE RANDALLS: SUMMER SKIES
May 2002
a special volume containing two additional
Brides for Brothers books:
COWBOY GROOM & COWBOY SURRENDER

RANDALL HONOR
July 2002
Victoria's story,
available from Harlequin American Romance

UNBREAKABLE BONDS
August 2002
a heartwarming original single title
from Harlequin Books

And look for more Randall stories from
Harlequin American Romance throughout 2002.

Dear Reader,

Once again, Harlequin American Romance has got an irresistible month of reading coming your way.

Our in-line continuity series THE CARRADIGNES: AMERICAN ROYALTY continues with Kara Lennox's *The Unlawfully Wedded Princess*. Media chaos erupted when Princess Amelia Carradigne's secret in-name-only marriage was revealed. Now her handsome husband has returned to claim his virgin bride. Talk about a scandal of royal proportions! Watch for more royals next month.

For fans of Judy Christenberry's BRIDES FOR BROTHERS series, we bring you *Randall Riches*, in which champion bull rider Rich Randall meets a sassy diner waitress whose resistance to his charms has him eager to change her mind. Next, Karen Toller Whittenburg checks in with *The Blacksheep's Arranged Marriage*, part of her BILLION-DOLLAR BRADDOCKS series. This is a sexy marriage-of-convenience story you won't want to miss. Finish the month with *Two Little Secrets* by Linda Randall Wisdom, a delightful story featuring a single-dad hero with twin surprises.

This month, and every month, come home to Harlequin American Romance—and enjoy!

Best,

Melissa Jeglinski
Associate Senior Editor
Harlequin American Romance

Judy Christenberry

Randall Riches

HARLEQUIN®

TORONTO • NEW YORK • LONDON
AMSTERDAM • PARIS • SYDNEY • HAMBURG
STOCKHOLM • ATHENS • TOKYO • MILAN • MADRID
PRAGUE • WARSAW • BUDAPEST • AUCKLAND

ISBN 0-373-16918-3

RANDALL RICHES

Visit us at www.eHarlequin.com

Printed in U.S.A.

ABOUT THE AUTHOR

Judy Christenberry has been writing romances for fifteen years because she loves happy endings as much as her readers do. A former French teacher, Judy now devotes herself to writing full-time. She hopes readers have as much fun reading her stories as she does writing them. She spends her spare time reading, watching her favorite sports teams and keeping track of her two daughters. Judy's a native Texan, but now lives in Arizona.

Books by Judy Christenberry

HARLEQUIN AMERICAN ROMANCE

*Brides for Brothers
†Tots for Texans

Don't miss any of our special offers. Write to us at the following address for information on our newest releases.

Harlequin Reader Service
U.S.: 3010 Walden Ave., P.O. Box 1325, Buffalo, NY 14269
Canadian: P.O. Box 609, Fort Erie, Ont. L2A 5X3

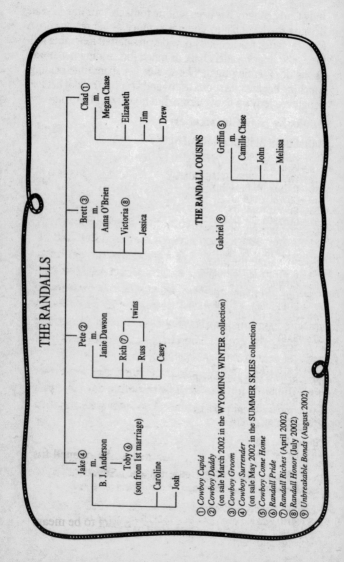

THE RANDALLS

Jake ④
m.
B. J. Anderson
Toby ⑥
(son from 1st marriage)
— Caroline
— Josh

Pete ②
m.
Janie Dawson
Rich ⑦
— Russ } twins
— Casey

Brett ③
m.
Anna O'Brien
— Victoria ⑧
— Jessica

Chad ①
m.
Megan Chase
— Elizabeth
— Jim
— Drew

THE RANDALL COUSINS

Gabriel ⑨

Griffin ⑤
m.
Camille Chase
— John
— Melissa

① *Cowboy Cupid*
② *Cowboy Daddy*
(on sale March 2002 in the WYOMING WINTER collection)
③ *Cowboy Groom*
④ *Cowboy Surrender*
(on sale May 2002 in the SUMMER SKIES collection)
⑤ *Cowboy Come Home*
⑥ *Randall Pride*
⑦ *Randall Riches* (April 2002)
⑧ *Randall Honor* (July 2002)
⑨ *Unbreakable Bonds* (August 2002)

Chapter One

Samantha Jeffers looked up as a rowdy bunch of cowboys piled out of the big booth. She'd waited on them, ignoring their flirting and serving them quickly and efficiently. She hoped they left a good tip, but probably not. The Hot Skillet wasn't exactly a high-class restaurant. But it did good business, especially when the rodeo was in town. She'd heard the winter traffic was good in this part of Arizona during ski season, but she'd gotten here right at the end of February, as the lifts were just shutting down.

As soon as the men were out the door, she went over to clear the big booth...and discovered the cowboys had left one of their friends behind. The man was slumped down, his face pale.

''Are you all right?'' she asked.

Slowly, as if his lids were too heavy, he opened his eyes. ''Yeah, sure,'' he muttered and closed his eyes again.

''Mister, the boss won't let you tie up this booth to sleep off your hangover.'' She wasn't trying to be mean, just stating the facts.

He opened his eyes again and sat straighter. The movement caused him to wince.

"Are you hurt?"

"Uh, maybe."

"Sam?" her boss called from behind the counter. "You gettin' that booth ready? There's a large party comin' in."

"I still have a customer," she turned and called over her shoulder.

"He orderin' anything?"

"Mister, you'll have to order something," she whispered, "or he'll throw you out for sure."

"I can't," he growled.

"Look, I'll cover the cost, but—"

"No. I think I have to go to the hospital."

Samantha frowned. "Mister, our food's not that bad." Her poor joke got a half smile out of him, which impressed Sam. He was obviously in pain. "Want me to call an ambulance?"

"No! I don't want anyone to know. My truck's here. I don't suppose you could drive me?"

Checking her watch, Sam realized she had fifteen more minutes of her regular shift, but she'd come in four hours early, at 6:00 a.m. this morning, as a favor for Brad, her boss. He should be able to spare her for fifteen minutes. "Wait a minute. I'll see."

She put down the big tray she'd carried to the table and crossed to the counter. "Brad, I need to leave fifteen minutes early."

He didn't look at her, a sure sign he was unhappy.

She'd been here a little over a month and had learned to read his moods early. "Not 'til your shift's over."

"Brad, I started at six this morning as a favor. Seems to me you could reciprocate."

"Don't use them big words on me!"

"You know what I mean. Anyway, it's not for me. That cowboy's sick. I'm going to drive him to the hospital."

"You mean you're gonna get in his bed. Don't lie to me!"

"Brad, that's none of your business. I do my job and I've done more than my share today. I'm going."

She turned away and he yelled, "If you leave, don't come back!"

She sank her teeth into her bottom lip and made a quick decision. She didn't like working here even if the tips were decent. And Brad had been trying to get a little too familiar lately. "Fine," she said calmly. "I'll clear out my locker."

RICH RANDALL FROWNED as he realized what had just happened. The waitress had just been fired because he'd asked for her help.

Now he regretted his ridiculous pride for not asking his friends, well, his semifriends, for help. He hadn't thought about the waitress's situation. She'd ignored all the horsing around of the guys while she'd waited on them. Hal had won the bronc riding at the rodeo. Rich had come in second to Jay in the bull riding competition. The whole group had been celebrating most of the day.

Before he could consider his choices, the waitress, pretty in a quiet way, came out from behind the counter, carrying a big pouch purse over one shoulder and a sweater over her arm. "Ready?" she asked cheerfully.

"Look, I don't want to cost you your job. We can call an ambulance."

"No need. Is your truck automatic or stick?"

"Are you sure?" he asked, trying to ignore the pain in his ankle and read her expression.

"I'm sure. Can you walk out of here?"

He'd make it up to her somehow he thought—when the pain eased. "Yeah, I think so."

She slid the table back, giving him room and then, as he stood, slid an arm around his waist. "Is it your leg?"

"My ankle. I—I must've sprained it."

"Which leg?"

"The right one. That's why I can't drive my truck," he said, still standing on his left leg, knowing when he shifted weight to the right one, he was going to be in even more pain.

"Let me get on the other side. Lean on me."

She had a slender build. Even at five foot six, which was what he guessed her height to be, she couldn't weight more than 110 pounds.

As if she read his mind, she said, "I'm stronger than I look. Come on. I want to get out of here before Brad loses his temper."

"He hasn't lost it yet?" Rich asked, thinking her sangfroid impressive.

She didn't say anything, but she started him moving.

The first time he put his weight on the right foot, he almost sank to the floor.

She straightened him up again and said, "I suggest you hop. Won't look too impressive, but that way we can get you out of here without you fainting."

Awkwardly, he complied with her suggestion. Each hop jarred the injury, but it was better than trying to walk on his right foot.

Outside, she paused for him to rest. "Okay?"

"Yeah," he managed to reply. "The black truck over there," he added, nodding at the line of vehicles to the right.

"Thank God you didn't park down the hill," she said, still smiling.

Rich was amazed at her good nature, but then she wasn't in pain like him. Her life wasn't in disarray like his. Her future couldn't possibly be as bleak as his.

"Here we go," she announced, her grip around his waist tightening.

Just a few more steps and he could rest. He gritted his teeth and hopped.

Five minutes later, he slumped against the side of his truck, exhausted.

"Your keys?"

"In my pocket," he said, panting but not moving.

"You mean you want me to get them out?" she asked. No more good nature. She sounded cold and unfeeling. "Look, cowboy, if this is just a come-on, you'd better find a better approach."

Rich stood there, his mouth hanging open, as she started walking away.

"Wait! I'm not—I didn't—" He reached out and lost his balance, falling, his cry hoarse with pain.

She came back to stare down at him.

"Damn it, do you think I could fake this? I'll find the damn keys," he assured her. She waited, saying nothing. He rammed his hand into the tight jeans pocket and found the keys, dragging them out. "Here. Satisfied?"

An agonizing moment passed before she bent over and helped him up. Then, without a word, she unlocked the passenger door of his truck. "Are you going to be able to get in there?"

He nodded. Even that movement brought pain. But he pulled himself up and in with his arm muscles. As he slid onto the seat, he was surprised when she lifted his right foot and gently placed it on the floorboard.

She disappeared around the truck, unlocked that door and climbed in. With ease, she slid the key in the ignition and shifted into reverse.

"You okay?" he muttered, fighting to stay conscious. The pain had gotten worse. He feared he would break into tears at any moment, and he'd be horribly embarrassed.

"How did you hurt yourself?" the lady asked after she had them on the road.

"A bull."

"You're a bull rider?" she asked. After he nodded, she said, "You're crazier than I thought. You landed wrong?"

"You could say that," he muttered wryly.

She pulled into the hospital parking lot and around

the side to the door marked Emergency Room. Instead of parking, she stopped at the door. "Stay put. I'll get a wheelchair."

He thought about it, but finally he nodded. There wouldn't be anyone here he was afraid would see him being wheeled into the hospital.

In almost no time, Samantha reappeared with a big, burly orderly and a wheelchair. The man pulled him out of the cab of his truck and eased him into the chair. Rich missed the waitress's feminine touch.

"I'll go park the truck," she said and got behind the wheel.

It occurred to Rich that the woman could drive off with his truck and he'd never see it again. "You'll come back, right?"

She chuckled. "Right."

SAM HAD PLENTY of time to think about her future. When she returned from parking the truck, she'd discovered the nurses had taken the cowboy, her cowboy, to X ray. Forced laughter came out. She didn't even know the name of the man who'd cost her her job.

No, that wasn't true. Well, it was true she didn't know his name. But she wasn't going to remain in that job much longer anyway. Brad, her boss, had been married four times, his most recent wife had died only a month ago. Suspiciously.

The sheriff had been hanging around. He'd warned her to stay away from Brad. She'd already figured that out. Brad, however, had been making noises about her stepping into the role of wife number five.

So now she had to decide where to go next. Flagstaff was a nice place, but she didn't want to be that close to Brad. It would be her luck that he'd turn out to be a stalker.

Motion nearby caught her attention. Two nurses were wheeling her cowboy down the hall.

"Hey! Is that you, cowboy?" she called.

He didn't answer, but one of the nurses did. "This is the man brought in a few minutes ago with a broken ankle."

Sam jumped up and stepped to the side of the wheelchair, walking with it. "Broken?"

"Yes. His walking on it didn't help the situation."

Slowly those brown eyes she'd seen earlier opened. "Too much noise," he muttered, obviously on pain medication.

Sam smiled faintly. He was most autocratic. She looked at the nurse. "What happens now?"

"That's for the doctor to say," the nurse said, suddenly prim and proper.

"Yes, it is," a man behind Sam said mildly as they pushed the wheelchair into a curtained-off area and moved the heavily sedated cowboy into a bed.

"Are you the doctor?" Sam asked the handsome man who looked about forty.

"Yes, ma'am. And you are…?"

"Samantha Jeffers."

He smiled. "Welcome to our hospital, Miss Jeffers. You did say Jeffers, not Randall?"

Sam shot a quick look at the cowboy. "Um, no, not Randall." Okay, at least she knew his last name. "Um,

I'm his fiancée,'' she hurriedly added, afraid she would be thrown out if she wasn't related to him.

''I see. Does he have any family here?''

Sam hoped she was doing the right thing. ''No, none. We were here with the rodeo. He's a bull rider.''

''Not a great career choice,'' the doctor said, sounding like he thought the man was an idiot.

She hadn't thought the cowboy was brilliant, either, but for some reason, she felt compelled to defend him. ''He's very good!''

''Well, it will be a while before he gets up on another bull.''

''How long?'' She knew Mr. Randall would want that question answered.

''Just a minute and I can tell you.'' The doctor turned his back on her and took a large envelope from the foot of the bed. He removed the negatives and put them on a lighted background. ''Hmm, he got lucky. It's a clean break.''

''So he can leave right away?''

''No. Because he walked on the ankle, the swelling is particularly bad. We're not going to put a cast on until the swelling goes down.''

''How long?'' Sam asked, feeling more concerned than she should have.

''A day or two. He'll need to keep the cast on for six weeks, probably. Then he'll be good as new. You worried?'' the doctor asked.

''A little.''

The patient groaned. Sam bent over him, brushing

back the dark hair that had fallen across his forehead. "You okay, cowboy?"

"It hurts," he whispered.

Sam looked up at the doctor. "Can't you give him something more for the pain?"

The doctor gave an order to the nurse and she hurried out of the room. "She'll be back in a minute with something to put him to sleep. He should stay asleep until morning."

"Thank you," she said, turning back to the patient. This was an unusual situation for Samantha. She had no family, no close friends. She'd never accompanied anyone to the hospital before. She hoped she never had to do so again.

"Do you need a ride home? Or a place to stay?" the doctor asked.

"No, but thank you for asking."

When the nurse returned, the cowboy barely opened his eyes to take the medication. Sam patted his arm and said, "I'll see you in the morning."

Then she slipped out of his room.

IT WAS ALMOST ten when Sam left the hospital. She drove by a fast-food place and got a hamburger to take home for dinner. "Home" was a room she rented from an elderly lady one block from the diner. However, before pulling up to her building, she drove past slowly, looking at the vehicles parked on the street.

As she'd feared, Brad's truck was parked right in front of Mrs. Walley's old house. Damn! He was waiting for her.

At least he didn't know she was driving the cowboy's truck. Tomorrow he'd go to the diner and she'd be able to slip into her room and gather her belongings. Thankfully, she traveled light.

She didn't have enough money with her to get a hotel room. Her savings were hidden in her room.

For tonight, she'd have to make do in the cab of the truck. She'd slept in worse places.

She drove to a nearby shopping center and stopped in the back of the parking lot. She made sure the doors were locked, put on her sweater and curled up on the truck bench seat. Thank goodness the cowboy didn't have bucket seats.

She awoke when the sun came up the next morning, a little sore from her constricted bed. There was a doughnut shop in the strip mall and she bought herself some breakfast.

She returned to the truck and started it up, praying Brad had left. But his car, a beat-up Chevrolet, was still guarding her room. She knew he was thinking she spent the night with the cowboy, which meant his anger was growing. She shielded her face with her hand and drove on by, then returned to her earlier parking space at the shopping center.

Knowing she was in for a long day, Sam went into the large economy store, bought herself a snack and a paperback book. She couldn't risk driving by her building too many times fearing Brad might notice the truck.

If Larry, his only cook, was handling breakfast, Brad would have to go in for the lunch crowd. So she'd have to stay hidden until eleven this morning. Then she could get to her stuff.

At eleven-fifteen, she parked the truck outside her room and hurried up the sidewalk. Mrs. Walley, her landlady, met her at the front door.

"Dear, you had a young man come calling last night."

Samantha shook her head, hiding a smile. The old lady was a complete romantic. No one else would describe Brad as a "young man." "What did he say?"

"He wanted to talk to you." Mrs. Walley peeked out the hall window. "I think he waited all night. He knocked on the door this morning and asked for you again, but I told him you hadn't come home. I don't think he was very happy."

"Mrs. Walley, I'm moving out today. Since I'm paid until the end of the month, you'll have some time to find another renter without losing money."

"Oh, dear, no! I've so enjoyed your being here. Must you go?"

"Yes, I must."

"What shall I tell that young man? Or will you talk to him?"

"No, I won't. Tell him I've gone to California." She gave the woman a brief hug and entered the place she'd called home for a little over a month. After checking out the window to make sure Brad hadn't come back, she took a quick shower and washed her hair.

Packing took about ten minutes. All her belongings fit in a duffel bag. She had to be ruthless with herself about what she kept. She couldn't afford to weight herself down with sentimental junk. A couple of changes of clothes, her toiletries, one towel. She used a spare T-shirt as her nightgown. Wearing her only pair of shoes, some athletic lace-ups, completed her sparse wardrobe.

She slipped out without talking to Mrs. Walley again and headed for the hospital. She suspected the cowboy was going to be annoyed that she hadn't stopped by first thing this morning. It had just been more convenient to pick up her belongings first. And she had to wait for Brad to give up.

It tickled her to drive by The Hot Skillet without Brad having any idea she was out there. The man was a bully. She felt sorry for the other waitresses who worked there and so very relieved she was no longer one of them.

THE PAIN greeted him as he swam to consciousness. Rich opened his eyes and recognized his hospital surroundings. He remembered his hardheadedness, his refusal to admit he was hurt to his so-called friends. The waitress who'd taken pity on him.

He looked around the room as if he expected her to be sitting beside the bed. Then he berated himself for such silliness. If his mother knew of his condition, she'd be here. She was the best. And his dad would chew him out, then give him a big hug. His twin, Russ…Rich's eyes filled with tears. Damn, he missed Russ. He even missed his baby brother, Casey.

He wanted to go home. Even if he wasn't returning as the conquering hero, as he'd imagined, he wanted to go home. As soon as the doctor released him, that's what he would do.

The nurse brought in his breakfast, giving him a cheerful greeting. She was young and pretty and he flirted with her. But he kept calculating how long it would be before the doctor checked on him…and how long it would be before the waitress came back.

"Anybody here to see me?" he asked as the nurse prepared to leave.

"I don't think so. Do you want me to check?"

"Yes, please. I'm expecting a lady, tall, willowy brunette."

The pretty little nurse looked disappointed, giving his ego a lift. "I'll ask," she said and turned to leave.

"Say," Rich said, stopping her again. "When will the doctor be by? I need to get out of here."

"In about an hour," she replied as she walked out of his room.

Almost to the minute she'd predicted, the doctor examined him and promised to put him in a cast that evening so he could leave the next morning. But he told him he couldn't drive for a month, even though he'd put him in a walking cast up to his knee.

Rich was devastated by that news. There was no way he was going to stay in Flagstaff for a month. Maybe he'd get the waitress to call home and get someone to fly down and drive him back. They'd have to come soon. His horse was stabled at the rodeo grounds, but they'd be closing the place tomorrow.

He spent the next three hours trying to plan a scenario that would get him home, get his animal taken care of and...with growing worries, figuring out what had happened to the waitress and his truck.

Just before they served lunch, the woman he'd become increasingly annoyed with finally walked into his room.

''Where the hell have you been!'' he yelled.

Chapter Two

"Sorry I'm late," the waitress said, seemingly unconcerned about his frustration.

"Where have you been?"

"Packing my belongings," she replied, moving closer to his hospital bed.

"Just like a woman," he said in disgust. "I'm lying here in pain and she's packing a huge wardrobe!"

She ignored his remark. "Has the doctor been to see you? What did he say?"

"He said I get out tomorrow. They'll put the cast on this evening, a walking cast."

"Great! You'll be all set, then."

"Not exactly. He said I can't drive for a month."

She seemed taken aback, which made him feel better. "What are you going to do?"

"Well, I've had plenty of time to work things out, since it took you so long to—what do you mean pack? Where do you think you're going?" He liked her. He appreciated what she'd done for him, but he hadn't expected her to pack her belongings and follow him home. What did she think she was doing?

She grinned. "Don't panic. My packing has nothing to do with you. I'm out of a job and—"

"Can't you find something around here?"

She raised one eyebrow. "I could."

"Then you wouldn't have to move," he pointed out.

"Thanks for the advice. Now tell me what you decided and where you want me to leave the truck."

"I need you to do a couple of other things for me if you don't mind. Can you go to the rodeo grounds and take care of my horse?"

"Your horse? You have a horse here with you?"

"Yeah." Why did she sound so surprised?

"You don't need a horse to do bull riding."

"I also do calf roping and team steer wrestling."

"Oh. Well, what do you want me to do with your horse? Do you mean clean out his stall and feed him? I can do that."

"I'm not asking you to do that kind of work. Check and see if Gabe Randall has left yet. If he hasn't moved on with the rodeo, get him to take care of Bella."

"Bella?"

"My horse."

"And if he's gone?"

"I'll give you some money to pay for someone to take care of her."

"Okay. For how long?"

"I don't know. I'll have to call home collect and explain. Explain what happened and ask someone to fly down here and drive me home."

"Where's home?" she asked, curiosity on her face.

"Rawhide, Wyoming."

He frowned when she didn't respond. She seemed to be concentrating, causing him to ask, "What?"

"Is Rawhide big enough to have some restaurants, a diner or something?"

"Sure. It's got just about everything…on a small scale."

"Then I'll drive you home, save you the cost of airfare."

Rich was suddenly uncomfortable. "Look, I appreciate the help, but I'm not offering— I just met you."

She stiffened. "All I offered was my driving ability, cowboy. Nothing else. Forget it. Where do I leave your truck after I see about your horse. At the rodeo? Is there someone I can leave the keys with?" She took several steps toward the door as she waited for his answer.

"Wait a minute! Don't leave yet." He didn't want her to leave. Had he made a mistake? The women who followed the rodeo, called buckle bunnies, took a little compliment and magnified it into a proposal or marriage if a man wasn't careful.

"Shall I wait until after you call so I can make arrangements for your horse?" She waited, but she didn't smile. She didn't look friendly, either. She looked more like she had last night when she thought he was conning her.

"Why would you want to drive to Wyoming?"

"I don't," she snapped, taking another step toward the door.

"Look, some of the women around here seem to think that if a guy pays any attention to her, he's offering something long-term. I didn't want to give you the wrong idea. I'll give you some money to carry you 'til you get a new job. I know I owe you that much, but—''

She fished the keys out of her pocket and said, ''I'll go get my bag out of the truck and then leave the keys at the desk in the emergency room. Good luck!''

She headed for the door.

''Wait!'' he ordered, but he wasn't really surprised when she kept going. He tried to swing his legs to the floor and fell with a cry.

She stopped and looked at him. Then she moved toward him. He smiled at her, expecting her help to get back into bed. His ankle hurt, but at least he'd stopped her from leaving. Instead, she punched the button for the nurse.

''Yes? How may I help you?'' A voice came through the intercom.

''Mr. Randall has fallen out of bed,'' she said calmly.

Almost immediately two nurses reached the door. They rushed to his side. He watched the waitress move to the door again. ''Please, don't leave! Make her stop, nurse!'' he pleaded.

''Ma'am, please wait. Surely you don't want to upset the patient.''

After staring at first the patient and then the nurse, she gave the conventional answer, ''Of course not,'' but he noted the complete lack of concern in her voice.

''Now, Mr. Randall, don't try to get up again or the doctor won't release you in the morning,'' the nurse warned after they had him settled.

When they left the room, he asked the waitress,

"Why would you be willing to drive me all the way to Wyoming?"

"Because I need to get away from here and it would save me the cost of a bus ticket."

Her simple explanation raised a few questions. "Why do you need to get away?"

"None of your business."

"It is if you've broken the law."

"Well, duh, if I'm a criminal, you don't want me to drive you anyway." She moved closer to the door again.

"Wait! Look, it would help me a lot if you'd drive me. I just didn't want—I mean—"

"I'm not expecting a wedding ring in exchange for two or three days' driving."

He drew a deep breath. "Okay, then I won't need to call my family. I'll call them when I get out of this place. But my horse… Hopefully Gabe will be there."

"Who is he? Family?"

"Yeah, kind of a second cousin."

"Why doesn't he drive you home?"

"Because he's on the hunt for the National Championship. He can't afford to miss a single rodeo. But he'll be glad to help with Bella if he's still in town."

"Fine. Is Bella hard to load?"

"No, but whoever you get to take care of her can load her for you, and hook up the trailer. Hand me my billfold, please. It's in that drawer," he said, waving her in the direction of the bedside table.

She opened the drawer and took out a leather wallet, then handed it to him.

He pulled out three one-hundred-dollar bills. Holding them out to her, he said, "You should be able to hire someone for a hundred, but if you need to pay more, you'll have it. Before you hitch the trailer up, fill up the gas tank. You might get us some drinks for the trip, too."

She stood there staring at the money. "Are you crazy?" she finally asked.

He frowned. "What are you talking about?"

"You don't hand over that much money to a stranger," she said, as if speaking to a child.

"You'll need it."

"I don't think so."

Frustration filled him. "Just take the damn money. And tell me your name."

"Samantha Jeffers," she said slowly.

"My name is Rich Randall," he replied, handing her the bills.

She took the money, folded it and slipped it into the pocket of her tight jeans. "I'll return what I don't spend."

"Fine. I should be ready to go by eight o'clock. You can make that, can't you? Since you've already packed." He regretted his sarcasm as soon as it left his lips. He needed her. It wouldn't be wise to insult her.

"I'll be here." Without another word, she left.

Rich leaned back against the pillow, feeling as if he'd just fought a battle. The woman was difficult. And he hoped he hadn't made a mistake.

GABE RANDALL WAS saying his goodbyes when Sam reached the rodeo grounds. She explained what had happened to Rich, and Gabe offered to stay an extra day to help him out.

She refused his generosity, explaining that Rich had told her that Gabe didn't have any spare time. She asked him to show her the feed and where to get water, and she'd take care of everything else.

Gabe did more than that. He showed her everything that would need to be done, and he introduced her to several men who worked at the barn. They agreed to help her the next morning.

"You've been very kind," Sam said, shaking Gabe's hand.

"Are you and Rich, uh, together?"

"No. I'm just helping him out."

"Well, Rich is a lucky man."

Sam figured she would be the one everyone would think lucky, if their engagement were real. The cowboy, like his cousin Gabe, was a handsome man.

"Do you have everything you need?" Gabe asked, seemingly reluctant to abandon her.

"Thanks to you, I do," she assured him.

"Well, I hope I'll see you again. I'll be stopping by Rawhide after the Nationals. Will you be there?"

"Maybe," she said with a grin.

"If Rich is as smart as I think he is, then I will be seeing you again. Tell Rich I hope he heals quickly."

With a frown, Sam asked, "Will he come back to the rodeo then?"

"Maybe. But I don't think so. I don't think his heart is in it." Then he shook her hand and walked away.

After Gabe left, Sam examined the trailer, hoping it was one of those that had a bed and storage at the front end. But no such luck. However, she could stay in the cab of the truck again, as she had last night. And the rodeo offered bathing facilities for the cowboys who stayed in trucks and trailers.

She made a run to a grocery store and bought some drinks and snack food. She also paid for a cheap blanket. It got cool at night in Flagstaff. But she knew it got downright cold in Wyoming. Then she drove to a gas station and filled the truck. When she returned to the rodeo grounds, she visited Bella. She'd been around horses a lot when she was little. Her father had made a little money following the rodeo and she'd cleaned stables alongside him.

Bella, she decided, was much sweeter than her owner. Sam and the mare became friends in the shadows as the light faded. Then she returned to the truck. With her new blanket, she settled down for the night.

RICH FOUND HIMSELF looking forward to Sam's return. Or did she prefer to be called Samantha? He seemed to remember the café cook calling her Sam, but Rich didn't think she liked the man too much. Maybe he'd ask her.

He was feeling much more congenial toward the waitress this morning because everything had been worked out. He was leaving the hospital. It wasn't a bad hospital, but he wanted out. He would be mobile again with his walking cast. And, most important of all, he was going home.

They brought in breakfast at seven. Rich enjoyed the scrambled eggs, biscuits and sausage. He figured it would save them a stop until lunch. If they pushed it, they might reach Rawhide late tomorrow. If they needed more time, they could pull in the next day at a reasonable time. It depended on what the driver could handle.

He was just finishing breakfast when Sam walked in. "You're early," he exclaimed.

"I thought you might be anxious."

He grinned. "Yeah, I am." He punched the nurse's button. "Hey, I'm ready to go. What do I have to do?"

"The doctor will be there soon," the disembodied voice assured him.

He scowled at Sam. "Did everything go all right?"

"Yes."

"Gabe took care of everything?"

"Yes," she repeated, smiling but reserved.

"You're not a big talker, are you?"

"No."

He stared at her, wondering if she was normally so taciturn. She'd seemed friendly enough the night she'd brought him to the hospital. Since then, they'd been at odds most of the time.

"Did you get breakfast?"

This time she nodded, just as the nurse came in to collect the breakfast tray. "Doctor just came on the floor, so he'll be here any time now."

Rich thanked her. After she left, he got up to visit the bathroom.

"Can you make it?" she asked, taking a step forward.

"Yeah. I'll be right out."

The nurses had slit the right leg on his jeans, which made it easy to get them on. He'd have to see if his mom could sew the seam again when he got the cast off since these were his favorite pair of jeans.

He came out of the bathroom just as the doctor entered the room. "Hey, Doc, I'm ready to go."

"I can tell. Good thing your fiancée is here to drive you."

Rich came to an abrupt halt, staring at Sam. She gave him a cool stare, not bothering to explain. "Uh, yeah."

"You remember you're not to drive for four weeks," the doctor reminded him.

He gave a nod but said nothing, still watching Sam.

The doctor turned to Sam, too, and handed her a small bottle of pills. "These are pain pills. He's going to suffer some before things get better. Be careful with these, they're pretty strong. Don't overdo them."

"No, I won't."

"I should be in charge of those," Rich protested, holding out his hand.

Sam slipped the bottle into her purse. "Is there anything else, Doctor?" she asked, ignoring Rich.

"Yeah. He'll be more comfortable if his leg is elevated. And he should see his own doctor when he gets home."

"Of course. I'll remind him," she said and gave the doctor a smile that lit up her face. Rich hadn't gotten that kind of smile.

"That's it, then," the doctor said. He held out a hand

to Sam and, in Rich's mind, held it too long. Then he shook Rich's hand. "Good luck."

Sam didn't move until the doctor had gone. "Ready? I'll get your jacket."

A nurse came in with a wheelchair. "Here we are, Mr. Randall."

"I have a walking cast," he pointed out.

"Good for you. Get in."

"But I—"

"Hospital rules," the nurse said, her manner firm.

He ignored the smile Sam was giving him and sat down in the chair.

She said, "I'll go ahead and pull the truck around to the door."

As she hurried ahead of them, the nurse said, "Pretty girl. When are you getting married?"

"We're not!" Rich snapped.

"The doctor said she was your fiancée."

"No, she's a friend." He needed to ask Sam about how the doctor had gotten the idea that they were engaged. But first he needed to get out of the hospital.

The nurse wheeled him outside and up to the truck. Once he was inside, Sam drove to the back of the parking lot and stopped. "Do you want to check on Bella?"

"Yeah." Had he been that obvious? Or did she understand about cowboys and their horses? He didn't know, but he was glad she'd stopped. He hobbled out of the cab and checked the connection between the truck and the trailer. Then he opened the trailer and tested the halter Bella was wearing.

"Everything is fine," he pronounced to Sam. "I should have known since Gabe took care of it."

Sam said nothing.

Once he was back inside, Sam pulled out a map. "I assume we'll be going east on—"

He stopped her. "No, we're going north, through Utah, into western Wyoming." He pointed out the route he wanted to take. "Okay?"

"Whatever you say. I'd like to stop and buy you a couple of pillows. It will make the ride easier."

"I don't need them," he replied.

Showing no emotion, she said, "Whatever you say," repeating a phrase that should've pleased him. They settled into the truck and she started the motor.

"Where were you going to stop for pillows?"

"There's a shopping center on the next block."

She didn't urge him again to consider pillows. Finally, he said, "We might as well get a couple of pillows. Thanks for thinking of it."

"No problem."

She pulled into the economy store's parking lot. "Do you need anything else?" she asked, as she reached for the door handle.

"Did you get drinks?"

"Yes, they're in the back. I'll get a couple out when I get back."

He watched her trot across the parking lot, wondering why she was irritating him. What she said had been perfectly polite, accommodating.

She returned with two pillows and cases to cover them. She removed the plastic and slid them into the cases and handed them in to him. Then she grabbed a six-pack of sodas and put them on the floorboard.

After she got in the truck, she told him to undo his seat belt and move to the middle of the seat.

"Why?"

"Well, since your right leg is the one hurting, we need to put it on the seat."

He insisted on putting the pillow against the door and putting both his feet on the seat next to her. She didn't argue. She took the other pillow and put it under his foot. Then she got a soda and opened it, passing it to him. He assumed they were ready to go, but then she pulled the pills the doctor had given her out of her purse. "Take this," she ordered, handing the small pill to him.

"I don't need it," he said.

"You're already hurting. There's no need to suffer."

With a sigh he took the pill, then sipped some soda. "Fine."

She didn't reply.

Once she started the truck, he relaxed against the door. The pillows had been a good idea. He began to feel bad about his difficult behavior. He noticed The Hot Skillet ahead. Thinking to make up for his boorishness, he said, "We can stop at the restaurant so you can tell your friends goodbye."

"No!" she replied sharply. "No, thanks, that's not necessary."

"Why not?"

"I don't want them to know where I'm going."

"You didn't take anything you shouldn't have, did

you?'' He regretted the question. Her face paled and her jaw tightened.

"No."

"I didn't mean—" He broke off, remembering why he was still wary of her. "Hey, why did the doctor call you my fiancée?"

Chapter Three

"You sure must be popular with the ladies," Samantha said, not directly answering his question. "Relax and go to sleep. I promise I won't marry you while you're napping." Okay, so she shouldn't be sarcastic, but she was tired of this man accusing her of something.

"I didn't mean to sound so suspicious," he apologized, turning on the charm. "But a man gets alarmed when he's told he's engaged to a stranger. An attractive stranger, I'll admit, but still a stranger."

"Like I said, you don't have to worry. I'm not looking for a husband. Just a ride. So you can save your cowboy charm for someone more susceptible."

He chuckled, even as his eyelids began to droop. "You think I'm flirting?" His voice grew softer, a little slurred.

Sam watched him out of the corner of her eye until she was sure he was down for the count.

It wasn't the first time she'd been falsely accused, though no one had ever suggested she was trying to trick a man into marriage. She'd discovered the newest person on the job had to walk a straight line or all kinds of sins would be heaped on her head. She kept her gaze on the road and he remained silent also.

A couple of minutes later, he gave a little snore. She gradually relaxed. It took energy to resist that charm she'd accused him of using.

At least she didn't have to worry about Brad anymore. He had no idea where she was now. Thanks to Rich Randall. She looked at him once again noting how handsome he was. Frowning, she turned back to the road. He looked familiar, but she knew she hadn't met him before.

With a shrug, she shoved that thought away. The less she looked at him or talked to him, the better off she'd be.

RICH SLEPT all morning. He awoke a couple of minutes around two when she stopped to fill up. She'd grabbed herself a hot dog while she was paying the bill. As she started to leave the station, she thought she ought to buy one for Rich, too. If he didn't want it, she'd eat it. Breakfast seemed a long time ago.

When she got in the truck cab, he was awake, frowning.

"Is your ankle hurting?"

"My ankle and my head. Where are we?"

"We're in Utah. Want a hog dog?"

Still frowning, he sat up a little bit, reached for the hot dog with a thanks, and ate it quickly.

When Sam held out another pill, he intended to refuse it, but the annoying pain had him reaching for it. Two minutes later, he was sleeping again.

Samantha waited until he'd nodded off to eat her own hot dog. Then she nursed her soda, making it last as she headed down the road again. She'd checked Bella's water while the truck filled, and the horse had seemed to be all right.

She decided she'd need to watch for a horse motel when it got time to halt for the night. Rich hadn't mentioned any place, even though he'd obviously driven this route before.

But she was pleased. Flagstaff was behind her. And a new life was ahead of her.

JUST THEN, the phone rang at the Randall home in Rawhide, Wyoming.

"Jake, is that you?" a voice asked when Jake Randall picked up the phone.

Jake knew he should recognize the voice of the caller, but he couldn't quite place it. "Yeah, who's this?"

"It's your cousin, Gabe."

"Gabe. How are you? Rich said you were in the hunt for the Nationals."

"I'm doing okay. Listen, is Pete there? I need to speak with him."

Jake waved to his brother, sitting at the table, a cup of coffee in front of him. "Here's Pete."

Pete took the phone. "Gabe? How are you? Are you coming our way?"

"No, sorry. I'm heading for California. I just wanted to check on Rich. He has called you, hasn't he?"

Pete felt his heart clutch. "What are you talking about?"

"Ah. He didn't call. Well, I hope I did the right thing. A young lady stopped by the rodeo grounds yesterday, she was driving Rich's truck. She asked me to show her what needed to be done to load up Bella. Seems Rich had a bad fall Sunday. He was in the hospital, she said. A broken ankle."

"A broken ankle?" Pete exclaimed, catching the attention of everyone sitting at the kitchen table. Especially Janie, his wife.

"Yeah. I tried to call him at the hospital afterward. I was a little worried, but there was no answer. That's why I thought I'd check with you."

"Well, thanks for the heads-up, Gabe. I'll check things out. Good luck this week. And come see us when you can."

"Will do. Hope everything's all right with Rich."

Pete hung up the phone. His wife, Janie, was beside him, her eyes big. "Now, honey, don't worry. I'm sure everything is fine," he said at once, as if he weren't worried.

Pete's three brothers and their wives were all there when the call came and all started firing questions.

Holding up his hand to stop their questions, Pete returned to the table and sat down beside Janie. "Now, a broken ankle is nothing. I mean, it will stop Rich's career for a while, but I'm sure he'll be all right."

"But why hasn't he called?" Janie demanded.

"Because he's a man and he can take care of himself," Pete assured her.

"But he won't be able to drive home," Jake pointed out.

"I know. But he's got a friend with him." Everyone relaxed as he added, "I'm sure she'll drive him home."

Janie stiffened. "She? His friend is a woman?"

B.J., Jake's wife, chuckled. "Are you surprised? Rich has always attracted the ladies."

"Yes, but I—I want him to marry someone from around here, not some—some rodeo floozie!"

"Now, Janie," Pete said soothingly, "Gabe said she was a friend. He would've said something if the woman was, uh, something else."

Jake leaned forward. "Yeah, you can trust Gabe, Janie. He's family."

They hadn't really known Gabe long, but he'd clicked with the men in the family at once. His father, a cousin of their father, had lived in Kansas City. Gabe's father and his wife had been to visit after their honeymoon. They'd planned another trip, but he'd been in an automobile accident and had died. Their father had gone to the funeral and offered the widow a home with him and his boys. But she was pregnant with Gabe. She'd chosen to remain in Kansas City.

She came to see them one more time, when Gabe was six, but she'd been a sad woman. She remarried when Gabe was eight. Then she'd died when Gabe was twelve.

They'd lost track of Gabe until Toby, Jake's oldest, went on the rodeo circuit. Since then Gabe had visited several times. He'd even discussed the possibility of making Rawhide his permanent home.

"What can we do?" Janie asked, drawing Pete's attention back to his son.

''I don't know. He's not carrying a cell phone. I'll call the hospital and make sure he was there.''

He returned to the phone with everyone watching. When he finished the call, he told Janie that Rich had been released that morning with a walking cast. ''The nurse said his fiancée was there to drive him home.''

''Oh, no!'' Janie exclaimed, covering her face with her hands.

RICH STRUGGLED awake, something nagging at him. When he opened his eyes and saw Sam driving, he tried to sit up and groaned with the effort.

She glanced over at him. ''You're awake.''

''Sort of,'' he said, shaking his head, hoping to rid himself of the grogginess he felt.

''How are you doing?''

''I don't know. Where are we?''

''Right at the border of Wyoming. I'm looking for a horse motel for Bella, but so far I haven't found one.''

He pulled himself up to look out the window. ''There's one about two more miles, next to a hotel. Nothing fancy but clean.''

''Good.''

When she didn't say anything else, he asked, ''How's the trip going?''

''Fine.''

''You want to add any details to that answer?'' he asked, exasperated.

''I've filled the truck up twice. I've checked Bella each time. I'm tired. Want to know anything else?''

He shook his head and sighed. "Sorry I slept so long."

"There wasn't anything for you to do."

"I could've kept you company," he pointed out.

"I'm not much of a conversationalist."

No kidding. "Hey, you never answered my question about why the doctor thought you were my fiancée," he suddenly remembered. This time he was getting an answer.

"I was afraid they'd toss me out of the room when the doctor asked me if I was family. I didn't think I'd pass for your sister. It seemed the best thing to say."

A simple enough explanation. He should've figured it out himself, but he'd been jolted by the doctor's statement.

"I see."

"You're paranoid about women, aren't you?"

He shrugged. That wasn't a subject he wanted to discuss with her. "Hey, where are you from? You got family somewhere?"

"No."

He stared at her. "You don't have family?"

"Not that I know of. But it doesn't affect my driving."

"Cute," he drawled. "I didn't say it did. I was just surprised. So where are you from?"

"My birth certificate says Dallas, Texas."

He shifted his weight and winced.

"You in pain? Need another pill?" she asked.

"No, I don't need another pill. Do you hate conversation that much?"

"I was concerned," she muttered and turned on her blinker. "I assume this is the horse motel you were talking about?"

"Yeah. I bet Bella will be glad to get out of the trailer."

"Probably. You go make the arrangements and I'll get her out."

He frowned. "You'd better let me. She's not used to you."

"Why not? I put her in there this morning."

"I thought Gabe put her in?" he asked in surprise.

"No, he left yesterday. I just barely caught him."

She stopped the truck and opened her door.

"Wait a minute. Why did you load her? I thought you were going to hire someone. Why didn't you?"

"I hired a couple of guys to help me hook up the trailer. But Bella is beautifully mannered. I didn't need any help for that."

"But I—"

"If you're worried about the money, I have it." She slipped out of the truck and dug into one of her jeans pockets. "Here it is. I used some to buy the pillows, too. And the gas."

He looked at the bills she handed him. Two one-hundred-dollar bills were there.

"What did you pay the guys for hitching up?"

"Fifty to split. Too much?"

He shook his head. "Nope. A bargain."

She said nothing, heading to the back of the trailer.

He got out and started toward the office, but he looked back to see if she could manage Bella okay. She was right about Bella's manners…if she liked the person. If not, she could be difficult. But she was on her best behavior today.

No wonder. Sam was petting and stroking her, using that sexy voice. He recognized envy in his thoughts. Ridiculous! All he was interested in was getting home.

Inside, he paid for Bella's stay and then went out to help Sam put her in a corral and toss her some hay.

"We can get rooms next door," he pointed out as they left Bella.

"She'll be safe?"

"Yeah. There's someone on duty all night."

She got behind the wheel of the truck and drove the few yards to the hotel. There was a café attached that had decent food. After dinner, Rich was looking forward to stretching out on a soft bed that didn't move.

"After we get the rooms, we can eat in the café." He was sure she was tired, too. She'd driven over ten hours without many breaks.

"I don't need a room."

He frowned. "Of course you need a room."

"I don't want to spend my money on a room."

"It's my money you'll be spending," he pointed out.

"No, I won't. I pay my own way."

"Consider it pay for doing your job," he said, sure that would settle the matter.

"No."

"What's wrong with you, woman? You expect to camp out?"

"No. I'll sleep in the cab of the truck."

"Don't be ridiculous!" He was becoming perturbed. "You'll be uncomfortable."

"I wasn't the past two nights." She slung her shoulder bag onto her shoulder and got out of the truck. "I'll save you a seat in the café." Then she closed the truck door and walked toward the restaurant.

He sat there with his mouth open. The last two nights? He'd assumed she had an apartment somewhere. Why hadn't she used it? When he realized he was wasting time, he marched inside the hotel and got a room. He checked to be sure they had more rooms in case Miss Hardhead changed her mind.

Then he strode toward the café next door. He was glad it was close. Even though he had a walking cast, his ankle still hurt every time he put weight on his right side. But he walked quickly.

Sam was sitting in a booth, the hair around her face damp. When he appeared at the table, she asked. "Is decaf coffee all right?"

"Yeah, fine. I'm going to wash up."

When he got back, the waitress was chatting with Sam. He slid in the booth.

"Do you need some time, honey, to check the menu?" she asked.

"Nope. I'll take a cheeseburger with fries, and a big piece of apple pie afterward. They have good pie, Sam."

"I've already ordered," she said calmly.

"Did you order pie?"

"No."

"Bring her a piece of pie, too," he said to the waitress. The woman looked at Sam, and she shook her head, still smiling.

Then she looked at Rich. "I can order for myself, thank you."

He considered fighting that battle. Then he decided she was right. She had the right to order for herself. Besides, he wanted some answers to his questions.

When the waitress left, he asked, "What do you mean you slept in the truck the last two nights? Why? Didn't you have your own place in Flagstaff?"

"Yes."

"Then why didn't you sleep in your own bed."

She took a drink of water. He noticed she hadn't ordered a soda or coffee. "I couldn't."

"Why not?"

"Brad was there."

His stomach clinched. She had a boyfriend? Or a husband? "Who's Brad?"

"The owner of The Hot Skillet."

"The one who fired you?" he asked, frowning. "You lived with him?"

"No."

"Then why was he there?"

"He was parked outside."

The waitress returned with his cheeseburger and a chef's salad for Sam.

"That's all you ordered?"

She looked surprised. "Yes."

"You and Brad had a thing going?"

"No. His wife died last month."

"His wife? I don't get it. Why was he there? And why did that mean you couldn't go home?"

"He'd decided I should be wife number five."

"His wife died a month ago and he's already looking for his next wife?"

"Yes. And I didn't cotton to the idea especially since it seems his wife died under suspicious circumstances. I slept in the truck so he wouldn't find me." She took a bite of salad. "He stayed until eleven the next morning, so I couldn't get to my things until he left."

"Why didn't you call the police?"

"It was easier to wait."

She continued eating as if they'd been discussing the weather. He sat silently, thinking about what she'd faced alone. Did it happen often? She was certainly attractive.

"I'm sorry," he finally said.

"For what?" she asked in surprise.

"I was rude about you taking so long to pack. Where is your luggage, by the way?"

"I put it in your storage trunk in the back of the truck when I loaded your gear. I hope you don't mind."

"There was enough room?"

She nodded, but it was the smile on her lips that fascinated Rich.

"What's funny?"

"Nothing."

"So Brad is the reason you decided to leave town?"

She nodded again.

"But your friends—"

"I'd only been there since the last of February, Rich. It's no big deal."

"But what if you can't find a job in Rawhide?"

She smiled again. "Don't panic. I take care of myself. If I can't find a job, I'll move on."

Once, when he'd been irritated with his parents, and even his twin, Russ, he'd wished he didn't have a family, that he could be all alone. In his juvenile imagination, he'd thought that would be a good thing. Now, he ached for the woman across from him. No family. No friends. Totally alone, no one to rely on.

"That's a tough life."

She shook her head, still calm. "It was worse when my father was alive."

"Worse? How?"

She sighed, then nodded at his plate. "You'd better eat your cheeseburger before it gets cold. Besides, I think you're going to need another pill tonight."

"No, I don't. Two in one day is enough."

"I'm not sure."

He realized she'd distracted him from her strange answer. He couldn't imagine life without his father and mother, his brothers, his huge family. They all lived on the ranch outside Rawhide. Well, actually, some of his cousins were down in Laramie attending college. But there were still a lot of Randalls around.

"When did your dad die?" he asked, after taking a bite.

"When I was sixteen."

"So...last year?"

"You think flattery will get you whatever you want, don't you?"

"It doesn't hurt."

"I guess not," she agreed, but she didn't say anything else.

"Okay, I'll be more direct. How old are you?"

"None of your business." She said the words pleasantly, but Rich could hear the steel in them.

"Why are you so secretive?" he demanded.

"Because you're not a friend. I hardly know you. It doesn't pay to tell your business to strangers. I'm driving you to Wyoming. That's it. I'll be on my way tomorrow after I get you home."

He didn't like the thought of that. She was too pretty and young to wander around without any protection. But she was right about him getting tired. He decided to talk to her about the dangers of her lifestyle tomorrow in the truck. They'd have plenty of time.

The waitress arrived with his pie. He ate it slowly, finding himself filled up on the cheeseburger. But he had to finish it after making a big deal about it to Sam.

As he took the last bite, the waitress returned with their bill. He was surprised but relieved when Sam didn't reach for the ticket. At last, she was accepting his providing for her. Next, she'd agree to take a room.

Looking at the total, he called the waitress back. "You forgot to put her salad on the bill."

"No, sir. She paid before you got here."

He glared at Sam. "You did what?"

"Let's not argue in front of everyone, Rich." She

slid from the booth, thanking the waitress again. Rich noted she'd left some money for a tip.

He handed the waitress a twenty and told her to keep the change. He knew they didn't do much business.

Then he hurried after Sam, catching her arm to stop her outside. "Why did you pay for your food yourself?"

"I told you I take care of myself. I handled it like that because I knew you'd make a fuss."

"Woman, you're trying my temper!"

"I'm tired, Rich. Just go to bed."

"Come on, then. They've got enough rooms. I'll get you one."

"No. I need to save my money. I'll sleep in the truck." She pulled her arm out of his clutches and headed for the truck.

He stared after her, unable to believe she could be so hardheaded. Then she stopped and turned around, coming back to him.

"I forgot." She pulled the pills out of her pocket and took one out. "Here's a pill, in case your foot starts hurting. What time do you want to leave in the morning?"

"I suppose eight o'clock. We're about eight or nine hours away. Unless you're too tired to get up that early."

"That will be fine." Then she walked away.

Rich stared after her, frustrated. He didn't have a sister, but he had girl cousins. And he wouldn't let any of them sleep in the truck when there were empty rooms available. But he had no choice. He could rent every room available and it wouldn't matter. Sam was going to sleep in the truck.

What was he going to do with her?

That was something else he'd worry about tomorrow.

Once in his room, he undressed and stretched out on the bed. His foot was throbbing. After a moment's debate, he decided to take the pill Sam had given him. He'd cut back tomorrow.

After swallowing the pill, he reached for the phone and dialed home, wanting to give his parents warning of his imminent arrival.

His mother answered. "Rich! How are you?"

"Fine, Mom. I'm fine."

"Don't lie to me, young man. Gabe called us."

"Ah. Well, I had an accident. I broke my ankle, but it will be good as new in six weeks."

"Oh, dear. Is it painful?"

"It's not bad."

"Where are you?"

"I'm on the Utah-Wyoming border. I'll be home tomorrow."

"You're not driving, are you? Gabe said your fiancée was with you. Have you got something to tell us?"

Rich rubbed his forehead. He was feeling very groggy. "Uh, no. Just Sam."

"What?"

"Just Sam," he said again. But he noticed he slurred his words.

"Rich? You don't sound good. Are you all right?"

"Took my medicine."

"Is—is that woman with you?"

"No, just Sam."

"Tell him to take good care of you."

"Yes, Mom. Gotta go."

He replaced the receiver, falling into a deep sleep the minute he closed his eyes.

Chapter Four

Samantha knocked on Rich's hotel room door the next morning. She'd gotten the number from the man at the registration desk.

She didn't hear any sound from inside. She pounded louder. "Rich? Are you all right?" Then she pounded again.

She decided to get the manager to open the door. As she was leaving, however, she heard a faint voice.

"Yeah?"

"Rich? Are you all right?"

"Yeah."

"Are you awake? It's seven-thirty. I'm going to the café for breakfast. Are you coming?"

"Uh, yeah. I gotta get dressed."

He must've taken the pill she'd given him last night. He sounded a little fuzzy this morning. "If you know what you want for breakfast, I can go ahead and order for you."

"Okay, coffee, a short stack, scrambled eggs, bacon."

And there wasn't an ounce of fat on him, she marveled. Not that she'd noticed, she assured herself. "Okay. Come as soon as you can so it won't get cold." Then she headed for the café.

The same waitress was on duty. "You worked last night and this morning, too?" Sam asked her as she sat down.

"I have to. My husband is sick. He lost his job. I'm the only one bringing in any money," the lady said with a weary smile.

Sam gave her their orders. She brought a pot of coffee to the table at once along with two clean cups.

Sam poured herself some coffee. She didn't often indulge, which made the times she did even more enjoyable.

She watched the waitress stop at another table. She often told herself she was better off without family. The waitress's situation reinforced that decision. She tucked the thought in the back of her mind to pull out when she got low. Sometimes she felt so totally alone.

Rich came in, still looking sleepy, dressed in those split jeans and a clean T-shirt. And he still looked good.

"Morning," she said cheerfully. But she didn't say anything else. She couldn't get used to having someone to talk to in the morning or she'd miss him tomorrow when she was alone again.

"Coffee," he muttered, reaching for the pot first thing. "Thanks for having it here."

"No problem. We have the same waitress as last night. She's working a double shift because her husband's sick and can't work."

He looked sympathetic. But instead of saying something, he studied her. "Have you already paid for your breakfast?"

She frowned. "No, but I figured you understood now." Darn, she should've taken care of it, but the waitress had distracted her.

"Ah. I'll leave a really generous tip if you let me buy your breakfast, too."

She stared at him. "She deserves a generous tip."

"She won't get one unless you cooperate." He sounded stern, as if he might really act so badly. She couldn't see any kindness in his gaze.

"That's ridiculous!" she exclaimed.

"Your choice," he muttered and sipped the hot coffee.

The waitress returned with a tray full of food. Most of it was Rich's. Sam had ordered a bowl of oatmeal.

"I forgot to ask about the ticket," the waitress said, as she put the food on the table. "Do you want it separated?"

Rich gave Sam a steady look, letting her know she hadn't answered his offer. She slowly shook her head. "No, the gentleman will be paying this morning."

With a nod, the waitress hurried away.

He smiled. "Good decision, Sam."

"Shut up. Blackmail isn't pretty!"

"I'm not sure the waitress would agree with you. I'd bet she's got some babies to feed."

She lowered her eyelids so he couldn't see the tears pooling there. She never cried in front of anyone. She couldn't afford to show a weakness. "I know."

Having broken one of her rules, Samantha felt nauseous. But she didn't dare not eat. She'd learned that lesson the hard way. She had to stay strong.

There was no conversation after that. As soon as she finished, she slid from the table. "I'll go load up Bella. You paid last night, didn't you?"

"Yeah. But I'll be finished in a couple of minutes and we can go together."

She turned around and walked out, not bothering to argue with him. He'd thought he could control her, but he had another think coming. She'd only succumbed this morning for the waitress's sake.

Of course, she wouldn't know how generous Rich was, because she wouldn't be there when he paid the bill. But, strangely enough, she trusted him to do what he promised.

When she pulled up in front of the café ten minutes later, Bella safely loaded, Rich strode out with two disposable cups of coffee.

He walked around the truck to the driver's side. She reluctantly rolled down her window. "Yes?"

"I got you some coffee for the road. I need to collect my gear from the room."

"Thank you. I'll wait here."

"Would you hold my coffee, too?"

She reached out and took it, settling it in the cup holder.

He started to walk away. Then he halted. "Oh, Paula said thank you."

Then he hobbled toward his room.

While he was inside, she carefully backed the truck and trailer close to his door so he wouldn't have to walk far. Then she killed the motor and got out to unlock the storage trunk in the back.

When Rich came out, she was standing beside the door and reached for his bag.

"What are you doing?" he asked in surprise.

"Loading your gear."

By the time he caught up with her, she was relocking the storage trunk. "Hop in. It's already eight o'clock."

"We're not punching a time clock, Sam. If we leave at eight-thirty instead of eight, it's no big deal."

She ignored him. Turning the key in the ignition, she put the truck in gear and pulled onto the road. She didn't touch her coffee until she had the truck going at top speed, where there would be no more shift changes. Then she removed the lid to her cup and took a cautious sip.

"They make good coffee," Rich said, sipping his own cup.

Instead of commenting on the coffee, she asked, "How much did you give her?"

"One of the hundred-dollar bills. I told her I'd promised you. She wanted to come find you to thank you, but I told her it would embarrass you."

Relief and gratitude filled her. She hadn't expected him to be so generous. But she was pleased. It had been worth swallowing her pride. "Thank you."

"You're a strange woman, Samantha Jeffers. You didn't want to let me pay for a bowl of oatmeal. But for someone else, you'll accept a tiny bit of what you've honestly worked for. I owe you more than that, you know."

"More than a hundred dollars?" she asked, staring at him before she turned her gaze back to the road. "For two days of driving? I don't think so."

"Airfare would've been a lot more. Probably five or six hundred. Plus they would've been shorthanded on the ranch."

"Well, consider me paid. I don't charge that much. How far is Rawhide from your place?"

"Fifteen miles," he said, still thinking about what she'd said.

"Is there a lot of traffic on the road?"

"You worried about the drive?"

Sam didn't want to tell him she was hoping to hitch-hike into town. She figured he's fuss at her. But she hoped to get there before closing time. If she was lucky she might even get hired at once.

"Why did you ask that?" Rich asked, drawing her attention.

"I just wondered."

"You don't have to worry about getting back to town right away. We've got lots of room. You can rest up a day or two. And have the best meals ever. Red and Mildred can't be beat."

"Who are Red and Mildred?"

"Red worked for our grandfather as a cowhand, but when our grandmother died, Red raised my dad and his brothers. When all the boys settled down, Red married Mildred. She's B.J.'s aunt. She moved to the ranch when B.J. came to be our vet."

"How nice." She wasn't sure why he was telling her

this, but it kept him from asking her any more questions.

"Yeah, she and Red had a double wedding with Uncle Jake and B.J."

"B.J. is a woman?"

"Yeah, kind of like your name. If someone said Sam, I'd think he was talking about a man. Why, last night I— Uh-oh."

Now he'd definitely caught her attention. "Uh-oh, what?"

"Well, I called home last night and my mom— That is, Gabe had called and told them I was—we were engaged. Mom wanted to know what was going on, but I'd taken my pill before I called. Things got kind of fuzzy. I don't think I explained that we're just acquaintances. I'm not sure. I can't remember."

"Well you should certainly know by now that I don't want to marry you. I'll explain to your mother as soon as we get to your house."

"Hell, Sam, I didn't say you did. I was trying to prepare you for our reception." He glared at her.

She didn't want to think about the kind of reception she might receive if they were engaged, and his parents liked that idea. But as it stood, she would probably face some hostile people, especially his mother. "How many in your family?" she asked.

"Mmm, twenty-one, I think."

She gulped and turned to stare at him. "Twenty-one? My, your poor mother."

He, in turn, stared at her. "Why?"

"Well, having that many children would—"

"No, you've got it wrong. Mom only had three kids." He chuckled. "Wait till I tell Mom that one."

"But you said—"

"Honey, Mom only had three kids, me and my twin brother Russ, and Casey, our kid brother. Everyone else is a cousin or an aunt or uncle. And Mildred and Red."

"I meant, how many people would be at your home?"

"Well, they all live there, but most of the kids are in college now, so they won't be home."

"You all live together? The house must be huge."

"It is. But a few years ago, we built the bachelor pad for all us guys. We still eat at the big house, but we have our own rooms in the pad."

She stared down the road, not saying anything.

"What's wrong?" he asked, his gaze on her.

"It's a little overwhelming. I've dreamed about having family, but it never occurred to me that some people had a small country for a family."

Rich chuckled. "It all started when Uncle Jake, the oldest of the four brothers, decided someone needed to marry so there would be another generation of Randalls. He did some matchmaking for his brothers, Brett, Chad and my father, Pete. Dad married my mom, Janie. She was a neighbor. Chad married Megan, a decorator from Denver, and Uncle Brett married Anna, a midwife-nurse. Then, the three wives turned the table on Uncle Jake and he married Aunt B.J. She's a vet. And then they all had kids."

"And they all live together? Didn't any of them want their own place?"

"Nope. You know that expression about it taking a village to raise a kid? We had our own village. There was always someone around to keep an eye on us. And some of us learned the hard way that we had to mind any adult. Even in Rawhide, we couldn't get away with anything."

"So you left home and went to the rodeo so you could get away with whatever?"

"No. That wasn't the reason." His upbeat tone had changed to something darker.

His tale had been so happy, so perfect, his dark expression worried her. "What happened?"

He sighed. "It doesn't matter."

"You're the one who started this conversation. Did you start hating your family?"

"No! But Russ got a girlfriend and I felt…left out. It's juvenile, I know, but my feelings were hurt. Russ and I had always done things together."

"That must have been difficult," she said softly.

"Yeah. And I didn't value my family because I guess I'd always taken them for granted. When I got hurt, I realized how much I missed them. I'm ready to go home. I can be happy for Russ. Abby is a nice lady."

"Good for you."

"Yeah, it's good I finally figured out what's important. Don't you miss that?"

"What?"

"Not having a home, a family."

"It's hard to miss what you haven't had."

That raw statement stopped the conversation. She concentrated on her driving, hoping he'd sleep for a while. Her emotions were too raw, hearing about his family and his life, a life she'd dreamed of too many times.

RICH DIDN'T SLEEP.

He was concerned. He wanted to help Samantha. He really did, but he had no idea how he could do so.

Of course he'd ask his mother to find her a job. But even if they found a dozen jobs, Sam might not take them. In fact, she probably wouldn't. He figured she'd leave Rawhide real soon.

Not seeing her wouldn't take her out of his head. He looked at her out of the corner of his eye. She wore no makeup. She pulled her hair back in a ponytail. Her clothes were well-worn and inexpensive. Her nails were short and unpolished. But she fascinated him.

His cousins, the girls, wore jeans and T-shirts, too, but they worked on their hair for a quarter hour, at least. Their nails were manicured and polished. Even their toenails. They had their ears pierced and wore different earrings all the time.

In their closets, they had dress-up clothes, too. Fancy shoes. He was beginning to suspect Sam didn't have much more than he'd seen.

He wondered if she'd asked about the traffic near Rawhide because she was planning on hitchhiking back into town. As if he'd let her. But that worried him most of all. Keeping Sam safe. He didn't want her running into another Brad, wanting her, taking advantage of her.

Maybe he'd ask his dad's advice.

He wasn't asking Uncle Jake. He'd suggest Rich

marry the woman. He didn't intend to marry for a long time. He was only twenty-six. His father and Jake had both waited until they were thirty or so. Brett and Chad had married earlier. Because Jake had done some matchmaking. He was still fond of playing those games.

Of course he'd gotten caught in his own trap. After all his brothers had married, their wives had conspired against him. Not that Jake complained. He and B.J. were perfect for each other.

Rich leaned his head back on the pillow and closed his eyes. He was a little surprised at how tired he was, since he'd slept over ten hours last night. But it would pass the time.

When the truck pulled off the road about three hours later, he woke up. First he checked his watch. Then he looked at Sam. "What's up?"

"I'm getting gas. I hope you still have money."

"Sure," he said, frowning. Leaning toward her, he saw the gas tank registered half-full. "Is the truck driving okay?"

"Yes."

"So you just wanted to fill up?"

"Yes. Is that a sin?"

"Nope, but—"

"*I* have to stop. Coffee goes right through me!" she snapped, her cheeks flushed.

He grinned. "Well, why didn't you say so? I could use a pit stop, too." He chuckled as she glared at him. So independent, but embarrassed about having to stop. She was a character.

When he returned to the truck, she was waiting for him.

"What are we going to do about lunch?" he asked.

She stared at him. "It's not even noon yet."

"In half an hour. They've got some barbeque sandwiches inside. We could get some and eat while we drive. Or there are some picnic tables under those trees."

"All right, I can get them when I pay for the gas," she abruptly said and held out a hand for money.

"Naw, I'll get them. You stretch your legs."

She opened her mouth to protest, but he stared her down. He wouldn't let her get the sandwiches because he knew she'd use her own money to pay for hers. He headed back to the little grocery store. Inside he paid for the gas and four sandwiches. He added chips and cold sodas. Then he picked up a bag of Hershey's Kisses. He'd bet Sam didn't treat herself often. He added a couple of apples so he could say he chose healthy things.

She was leaning against the hood of the truck, watching him as he approached.

"Did you think we had a family of six with us?"

"What are you talking about?"

"It looks like you bought enough to feed a crowd," she said suspiciously.

"It'll help pass the time. And I want to have supper at home tonight, so we'll save time not stopping for more food."

He put the bag on the seat and reached over to get their coffee cups to throw out. Then he pulled himself into the cab. He took out the two sodas and put them in the cup holder. He settled back against his pillow as Sam slid behind the wheel.

"You sure you're okay with eating while you drive?"

"I'm fine," she said. "There's not much traffic out here. I'm going to need some directions later, so maybe it is best if you stay awake. How's your ankle?"

"Fine. You get started and I'll unwrap your sandwich."

She started the engine and pulled out onto the highway. Once she was up to speed, he unwrapped her sandwich and handed it to her. Then he opened a bag of potato chips and put it on his legs, between them. "Your drink is in the holder. If you can reach it, I'll open it for you."

"I can open it."

He covertly watched her eat. He liked knowing that he'd paid for her food. Silly, he guessed, but she needed a keeper. She would've probably tried to go all day on a bowl of oatmeal.

When she finished her sandwich, he reached into the bag and brought out the two big red apples. She took one of them, pleasure on her face. "Oh, I love these!"

He thought of women he'd dated and the expensive gifts he'd sometimes given them. None of them had looked as pleased as Sam when she saw the apple.

They seemed to have a cease-fire for the next few minutes as they both munched on the apples. But when he pulled the bag of candy Kisses out of the sack, after disposing of the apple cores, she glared at him again.

"You shouldn't have bought those. They're not good for you."

"You don't like chocolate? That's strange. I thought all women liked chocolate," Rich teased.

She refused to say another word, or to eat any of the candy. But he caught her looking at the bag occasionally, as if longing for it.

"Why won't you eat chocolate?" he asked.

"It's expensive."

"You think I'm going to ask you to pay for it?" he asked, incredulity in his voice.

"No. But you won't be there the next time I get a craving for chocolate. I can't spend my money foolishly. So it's best if I don't eat any. It's addictive."

Damn, he'd hoped to please her. Instead, it seemed he'd made life difficult for her. He put the bag of candy back into the sack so she couldn't see it. "Sorry."

"I didn't mean you couldn't—"

"Forget it!"

And that ended the conversation.

ABOUT FOUR O'CLOCK, Rich told her to turn off at the next gate she came to.

"You mean we're almost there?"

"About ten minutes away," he said with a smile.

It was the first smile she'd seen since she'd refused the candy four hours ago.

The next left was a gravel road that led to a gate with a cattle guard. "Are we on your ranch now?"

"Yep. Man, it's good to be home."

Samantha felt a trembling in her stomach. The trip

was ending. She'd be back on her own in a few minutes. It hadn't taken long to get used to having a companion, even if they didn't talk much.

She swallowed the lump in her throat. Moving on was hard until she'd found a place and settled in, knew she could make it. But that was her life. She accepted it.

They topped a hill, and down below, she saw a sprawling house with several enormous barns. "Big place, like you said," she commented. She'd figured his family was doing well, but not this well.

"It's a great place. I'll show you around after dinner."

"Thanks, but I've got to get to town and see what I can find in the way of work. I won't stay for dinner."

"Yes, you will."

She glared at him. "Haven't I convinced you that you can't order me around?"

"Yeah, but you haven't met my family. They can talk anyone into visiting. Mom will feel she owes you something for bringing her baby boy home." He grinned.

"You're not the baby of the family."

"No, but mothers always think all their children are babies. You know how it is."

"No, I don't."

He apologized again, but she waved the words away. "Don't worry about it."

He showed her where to park. By the time she'd stopped the truck, a crowd of people had piled out of the house, shouting Rich's name.

She'd never seen such a welcome, or even imagined such a family existed. Rich was occupied with getting out to greet them, and Sam took the keys to open the storage bin after she got Bella out of the trailer.

Bella seemed excited to get out, almost as if she knew she was home, too. Samantha patted her neck and looked for the nearest corral.

"Want some help?" a young man asked. He looked a lot like Rich.

"Can you tell me what corral to put Bella in?" she asked, smiling. He looked so fresh-faced and innocent.

"I'll take him. You probably want to go in and have something to drink, put your feet up. That was a long drive."

She had no intention of doing that, but she let him take the horse and lead her away.

"Sam?" Rich called.

Strange how she could identify his voice among all the noise. "Yes?"

"Come here. I want you to meet my family."

She guessed she couldn't escape introductions. She moved from behind the trailer, anxiety in her heart, though she tried to hide it.

The entire family must've been there, all staring at her. She lowered her eyes, wishing she were somewhere else.

Until someone called her name.

"Samantha? Is that you?"

Pure joy rushed through her. "Pete? Pete!" And she launched herself into Rich's father's arms.

Chapter Five

Rich stood there stunned. The woman with whom he'd traveled—the difficult, quiet, always reserved woman—was hugging his father. His father! Rich quickly looked at his mother.

Janie was staring at Pete, her husband and the young woman he was hugging, but she didn't seem upset. In fact, she was smiling.

What the hell was going on here?

He wasn't the only one wondering. Red spoke up. "I don't know what's going on, but why don't we all go inside and have some coffee?"

Sam seemed to immediately revert back to the solitary woman he knew as she moved out of Pete's arms and apologized. "I'm sorry. I didn't expect…I shouldn't have…I have to go."

This was the reaction Rich had expected.

"You'll do no such thing," Pete said insistently. "Let me introduce my wife, Janie. Honey, this is Samantha."

Janie beamed at her. "I guessed, or you'd be in big

trouble, young lady. I keep a close eye on my husband.''

Sam took another step backward. ''I didn't mean anything by it, I promise. But Pete is an old friend.''

Janie stepped to Sam's side and put an arm around her. ''I know that. He used to come home from the rodeo and talk about you. That's why we tried to adopt you.''

When Samantha's knees buckled at that statement, Rich wrapped an arm around her before his father could get to her side. Ridiculous idea, he and his father competing for the same woman. But Rich was going to be the one to support her, if anyone was.

''Aw, Janie, you shouldn't have sprung that on her,'' Pete said. ''She never knew.''

''I'm so sorry,'' Janie said.

At the same time, Red was rounding everyone up.

''To the house!'' the older man ordered. ''I gotta sit down.''

Rich, however, wanted some answers. ''What the hell is going on? Why didn't you say you knew my father?''

''I didn't know Pete was your father,'' Sam said, her voice shaking. ''I didn't know his last name was Randall.''

''Come on, son,'' Pete said. ''Bring her on in and we'll explain everything.''

Rich made sure Sam knew she had no option, his arm tightening around her as he started forward.

''Please,'' Sam whispered, ''I really should go.''

''You're not going anywhere until I get an explanation.'' He pulled her along with him, his mind in a state of confusion. He did notice, however, how well she fit against him.

They all walked inside, down the hallway and into the kitchen to sit at the four places left at the large table.

Mildred was busy setting coffee cups and a plate of cookies on the table. Everyone else was looking on at the four people who had just arrived. No one wanted to miss the explanation for what they'd seen and heard.

Janie took the first seat and Pete the one beside her. Rich wanted to sit between his father and Sam, but he wasn't given any choice. Pete pulled Samantha into the next seat, leaving Rich to sit at her other side.

"Samantha is—was the little girl I saw at some of the rodeos. I first met her when she was six. She was cleaning out stalls with her father."

"At six?" Red asked, frowning. "You mean, she'd help him every once in a while?"

"No, he'd assign her a stable and then go off and clean another one. She'd do the whole job by herself."

"That's not right," Mildred said. "That's hard work. Why, she wouldn't be old enough to handle a pitch-fork."

Sam remained silent, keeping her gaze on the table. Rich watched her closely.

"Yeah. I once tried to talk to her father about her. The twins were eight years old. Janie wanted a little girl, and I wanted Samantha to have a better life."

"I didn't know," Sam whispered.

Pete patted her hand. "I know, honey."

Rich's arm went around her chair. He wanted to be the one to comfort her.

"I looked for her every time I traveled to any of the rodeos. Sometimes I'd find her and sometimes I wouldn't. And whenever I did see her, it would break my heart to know she wasn't being loved enough. Then, a few years back, I heard her father had died and she had disappeared. I contacted the police, but they said social services couldn't find her." He cleared his throat. "Where did you go, Samantha? You were only sixteen."

She shrugged her shoulders, still not looking at Pete. "I started waitressing. It was a better job for me. The cowboys...they weren't all like you, Pete."

"I know, honey. So how did you end up with my son?"

Sam looked at Rich briefly, then said, "I wanted to leave town and offered to drive him."

They all knew there was more to the story, but Rich wasn't going to say anything in front of the entire family.

"You'll stay for a few days, won't you?" Pete asked.

"We'd love to have you," Janie added.

"Uh, I need to go. I—I've got a job waiting for me. But thanks for the offer." Though both Janie and Pete protested, Sam rose with a brief thank you and headed for the back door.

Rich intentionally didn't catch up to her until after she was outside. He grabbed her arm and spun her around. "It's not nice to lie, Sam."

"I can't stay here. Tell them it was sweet of them to offer. But I can't—"

"Why? You're an old family friend."

"No! I'm not. I'm a child your father took pity on. I have no place in his life." She pulled Rich's keys out of her jeans and headed for the truck.

"What are you doing?"

"I'm getting my bag."

Ah, the infamous luggage he'd accused her of taking hours to pack. But bag? One bag? He watched her as she opened his storage box and pulled out a duffel bag. Without another word, she slung it on her back and started down the long gravel drive.

Rich stood there, stunned. Her entire belongings in one duffel bag? He thought of all his clothes, his gear, mementos of different events in his life. He couldn't have fit it all in ten duffel bags. He realized he'd better hurry if he was going to stop her. With his cast, he wasn't as fast as he normally was.

His father stepped off the porch. "Where's she going?"

"I don't know. She doesn't have a job. Dad, everything she owns is in that bag."

"I think we'd better take the truck. I have a feeling she'll outrun both of us."

She'd left the keys on the floorboard of the truck. Pete grabbed them as Rich swung up into the passenger side. They caught up with Samantha quickly. Pete pulled around her and parked the truck. They both got out.

Pete caught Samantha by the arm. "Honey, I know the family is a little overwhelming, but I'm not sure I understand what the problem is."

She stared straight ahead. "I need to go."

"That much I got. But why?"

Rich watched her, saying nothing. Finally, she looked at him and muttered, "It's like the chocolates."

Suddenly he understood. She couldn't stay a few days because it would hurt too much when she left.

"Sam—" he began. But what could he say? Promise she could stay forever? He couldn't do that.

His father looked at Rich. "What's she talking about?"

Sam stood there, her head lowered, saying nothing.

Rich finally explained. "Sam's very disciplined. She doesn't want to stay with us because it will hurt when she has to leave." He cleared his throat because the thought was so disturbing.

"Honey, you don't have to leave," Pete said. "I tried to find you when your father died. I was going to bring you back here, offer you a home. The offer still stands."

"Pete, I can't!"

"Why not?"

"Because it's not fair to you…or your family. I can't just waltz in here and put my feet up. I have to earn my way."

"You can get a job, of course, but you could take a little vacation, couldn't you? Give us a chance to visit? Janie always wanted to meet you. The world's not going to run away if you pause for a few days, let us get to know you again."

"Your family—"

"Will be delighted. Right, Rich?"

"Uh, yeah." Rich stared at Samantha, irritated by the

warmth she showed his father, especially since she always pulled away the moment he got close.

"Come back to the house. Janie will have gotten a room ready for you. We'll get you settled in and eat dinner. We'll help you find a job. Everything will be fine."

"Are you sure, Pete? I can make it on my own."

"Of course you can. You have for the past eight years."

That information told Rich she was two years younger than him. Eight years she'd been out there struggling on her own. He doubted her father had left her anything.

"I'll stay the night," she agreed, lifting her chin.

Pete opened his mouth to protest. Then, with a smile, he said, "Good."

Rich watched the two people in front of him. He knew his father didn't want Sam to leave. And it wasn't often that his father lost a fight.

Samantha finally nodded and said, "Thank you for understanding, Pete."

"Come on, let's go get you settled in."

Rich followed along behind, feeling superfluous. For two days, he'd had Samantha to himself. But since they reached the ranch, it was Pete she turned to. Huh!

SAMANTHA PACED the bedroom she'd been given like a caged lion. Her hands shook and she was having difficulty thinking. She couldn't believe how seeing Pete again had affected her.

He'd been special to her for the longest time. It was

because of Pete that she didn't consider all men evil. Her father told her she had to earn her keep, or he'd get rid of her. When he discovered that some of the cowboys tipped her for "doing such a good job," however, he changed his mind. He'd forced her to give him the extra money.

She'd caught on quickly. Money was the key. She began hiding money from her father. She gave him enough to keep him from getting suspicious. The rest she kept hidden. She had over seventy-five hundred saved. And she continued to put aside everything she could.

Because that was all she had.

Pete had given her money. But he'd given her more than that. He'd talked to her, asked questions, told her stories. He'd been her only friend.

To see him again, without warning, had brought back such joy. She shouldn't have hugged him. And then for his wife to tell her they'd tried to adopt her. She closed her eyes, coming to a halt. To think she might've lived here, with family. But her father had obviously refused to give up custody of course, because she was making money for him. Even at the age of six.

She forced her eyes open and began pacing again. It would've been a dream come true. But it was too late. She was no longer a child. She could leave tomorrow. It wouldn't be so hard. And she'd know where to find Pete if she…well, she'd know where he was.

But that was as long as she could stay. The Randalls seemed to be a happy group of people, loving each other. They were so rich in—in family…rich in love.

Earlier, she'd met Jake and B.J., Brett and Anna, Chad and Megan, Toby and Elizabeth. All seemingly happily married. Then there was Russ, Rich's twin. They were identical, but she could tell the difference. Imagine having a twin. Someone you could always trust.

The boy who'd taken Bella and put her away was Casey, Rich's younger brother. He was still in high school, the youngest of the second generation.

They were the kind of family people wrote about. Not the kind of family she knew. And that was why she had to leave. She wouldn't fit in here. She couldn't. She didn't know how to trust. She didn't know how to enjoy life. Most important of all, she didn't know how to love.

THE FOUR ELDER Randall brothers and their wives stayed up that night after the other family members had gone to bed.

Jake sat at the head of the big kitchen table. "What do you think, Pete? Will she stay?"

Pete looked sad. "I doubt it. We're kind of an overwhelming bunch. Samantha's used to being alone."

"She's afraid to stay because it will hurt too much when she leaves," Janie added, having learned that from her husband.

"I can understand that," Anna said softly. "I never thought I'd fit in, either."

Brett, her husband, put his arms around her. "Aw, Anna, you were perfect. Still are," he added with a grin.

She gave him a little kiss and leaned her head on his shoulder.

"She might stay longer if she could find a job. But

that would be the only way. And she doesn't have a car, so work would have to be nearby," Pete said.

"We can always hire her to help Red and Mildred," B.J. said.

"She'd be suspicious about that," Pete said. "She's independent."

"But I can't stand the thought of her out there by herself," Janie said. "We need to be sure she's safe. I'm afraid we're a little too much for her but— Mom!" she exclaimed.

"What, Janie? What did you think of?" Pete asked at once.

"I told you Mom's getting lonely and depressed, over there by herself, but she won't move in with us. Too many people, she said."

"Yeah, but you've asked her about hiring some help and she doesn't want strangers around," Pete pointed out.

"But Samantha isn't a stranger. And I can explain to Mom that Samantha is uncomfortable with all of us."

Jake leaned forward, grinning. "You might also explain that her grandson's interested."

Pete's head snapped up. "Now, Jake, we'll have no matchmaking here."

Jake's eyes widened innocently. "I was just stating a fact, Pete. Ask the others."

Pete looked at his brothers. Brett shrugged his shoulders, but Chad was more vocal. "Hell, Pete, she's a good-looking woman. Straightforward, independent. And I'll admit I got the idea he wasn't too happy that you and she were so close."

"It must've been a shock to him," Anna said.

"I know you don't want to pressure them into anything," Megan began, "but it'd be a perfect solution."

Jake added, "You know, you were going to hire a new manager for your mother, too, since Sid quit last week. Seems to me that would be a good job for Rich, at least temporarily."

"Well, that's true," Brett said. "He could live there and keep an eye on the two ladies. And Samantha could drive him when he needs to go to town."

Janie looked at her husband. "Pete? What do you think?"

"I'm not sure Rich is ready for that big a job." As his brothers started to protest, he held up his hands. "I don't mean the job. I'm talking about his ankle. He had to take another pain pill tonight. Samantha gave them to Janie. Said the doctor warned about using too many."

Anna looked up. "How many did he take today?"

Janie answered. "Only this one. But he had three yesterday."

"Then he's doing fine." As a nurse-midwife, Anna was the medical expert on the ranch. "But Pete's right. He'll need to go slowly. Maybe keep him here at home for a week before you spring his grandmother on him. It will lull any suspicions he might have," she added, grinning.

Janie exclaimed, "We're really not matchmaking! We just want to keep Samantha around. I'd like to get to know her. Wouldn't hurt to have a little help for Russ's wedding, either. Since Abby's mother is dead, I'm going to be doing a lot."

"Yeah, and we want her to stay for the twins' birthday," Megan agreed with a grin. "Since Russ is getting married on his birthday, that means she'll be here for the wedding."

"I'm not sure she'll want to stay if we say anything about those things. She won't be used to big celebrations."

"Okay, we'll play on her sympathy to help us with Mom. Pete, you can handle that, can't you?" Janie asked, a twinkle in her eye. "You were always good about talking me into things."

"Were?" he asked, acting highly offended that she thought he might've slipped.

"All right, I'll go talk to Mom first thing in the morning and then you can approach Samantha at lunch."

"All right, but everyone's going to have to keep an eye on her tomorrow. She may try to leave as soon as she gets up," Pete warned.

In agreement, the couples went upstairs together, as they did most nights, to their own suites.

Once they were alone, Janie turned to her husband. "I hope it works, Samantha and Mom. Mom can be difficult now that she's all alone."

"Samantha's tough, honey. She'll be able to handle her. But we're going to have to be careful and not let on anything to Rich."

"We're doing the right thing, aren't we?"

Pete wrapped his arms around his wife. "We're trying to keep Samantha safe. There's nothing wrong with that. As for her and Rich, I'd be pleased, but we won't pressure them. If they don't get along, we'll find someone else for Samantha. I don't know about Rich. I'm not sure he's ready to put down roots.''

"Well, I think he is."

"Mothers always do," he said with a laugh.

"Do you think it was mothers who started the matchmaking? It's the men in this family who insist on matching everyone up!"

"Yep. And they've done a pretty damn good job!" he said before he kissed her.

When he raised his lips, Janie leaned against him. "Well, I didn't say I was complaining."

"I just want our sons to find the happiness I've had, sweetheart. And I'd like Samantha to have a chance, too. But I think Rich is going to have to be patient."

"Not always a Randall trait," Janie pointed out.

Chapter Six

Janie drove to her mother's home, the closest house to the Randalls', early the next morning. Though her mother could sleep late, she never did. Old habits die hard.

"Mom?" she called as she opened the back door.

"In here, Janie," Lavinia Dawson responded from the kitchen.

"How are you this morning?"

"Wondering if you've forgotten me," Lavinia said tartly, keeping her back to her daughter.

Janie hurried to the sink where Lavinia was working. "What are you talking about?"

"Well, I waited all evening for you to tell me Rich made it home all right. You never called."

"Oh, Mom, I'm sorry, but— Why didn't you call me?"

Lavinia lifted her nose in the air. "I didn't want to be a bother."

Janie laughed. "You must've fallen asleep early."

Lavinia had the grace to grin and nod. "But he did get home all right, didn't he?"

"Of course. About four o'clock. We gave him a pain pill last night, but I think he's going to be okay soon."

After a quick look at her mother, Janie went to the table and sat down. "It's who else arrived that stunned us and distracted me."

"He brought someone with him? A bride! Rich got married! He always was—"

"No. Rich didn't get married. He brought Sam with him," she said, deliberately teasing her mother.

"Another cowboy? What's surprising about that?"

"Not another cowboy. Do you remember me telling you about the little girl Pete used to see at the rodeo? Samantha? How we decided to adopt her, but we didn't get to?"

"Well, of course I remember. Do you think I'm feeble?"

Janie grinned. Her mother was very sensitive about her age. "No. But that's who Rich brought home with him."

Lavinia's jaw dropped. "You're kidding. How did he know?"

"He didn't."

"Well, my goodness. I can't believe that."

"I know. But Mom, she's been totally on her own for eight years. We don't want her going back out into the world by herself. It could be dangerous."

"Of course it could. Why don't you offer her a home?"

"We did. She stayed the night, but she's trying to leave as we speak. She told everyone goodbye when she came down this morning. Didn't think she should eat breakfast even.''

"Why?''

"She's very independent. Thinks if she accepts a favor, she'll have to pay it back. That's how a lot of the cowboys operated. She says she needs to be on her way to find a job. I'm afraid we're such a big crowd, we intimidate her.''

"Told you there was too many of you.''

"I want you to help us.''

"What can I do?''

"Pete's going to tell her you're getting too old to live alone, but you want to stay in your house. We'll hire her to help you out here.''

"I am not too old!'' Lavinia shouted.

"Of course you're not. But if Sam believes Pete, she might agree to live here with you for a while, until she gets to know us, to feel comfortable. And she'll be safe. She'll think she's taking care of you, but *you'll* be taking care of *her*.'' Janie paused before she added the kicker. "It would mean a lot to Pete.'' Pete was her mother's favorite Randall since he was also her son-in-law.

"I suppose I could. But is she a nice girl? What if she murders me in my sleep?''

"Mom, you know I'd never put you at risk. Samantha is worried about paying her own way. She doesn't want to take favors. If she were a con artist, she wouldn't worry about what we offer her.''

"Okay, I'll agree.''

"Thanks, Mom." Janie leaned over and kissed her mother. "There might be an added benefit."

"What's that?"

"Rich. He might be interested."

JANIE MET PETE in the barn as he swung out of the saddle. "Did she stay?" he asked first thing.

"Just until lunch. We told her you were counting on having lunch with her. Then one of us would drive her to Rawhide." She kissed him, then added, "And Mom agrees to play along with our plan."

"Great! Let's go see if I can talk her into it." He wrapped his arm around Janie and they started for the house.

"How's Rich?" he asked. "Has he gotten up?"

"Around ten. Those pills make him groggy. But he was doing better after a cup of coffee."

When they reached the kitchen, Pete noticed Samantha's duffel bag in the kitchen, probably so she could get away as soon as she'd finished eating. She was sitting at the table with Mildred, Rich and Red. The other men weren't coming in for lunch, and everybody else was about their business.

When Red saw Pete and Janie, he hopped up to carry lunch to the table. Mildred was going to help, but Samantha waved her back to her seat and helped Red.

"This here little girl is right handy," Red said.

That compliment brought a becoming flush to Sam's cheeks. Pete checked out his son to see his reaction. Rich was staring at her, but he quickly studied his coffee when he realized his father was watching.

"Good," Pete said. "I think she kind of decorates the place, too. Right, Rich?"

"Uh, yeah."

Once they started eating, Pete began his machinations. "Sam, we need a favor."

Her head snapped up, a wary look in her eyes. "What, Pete?"

"Janie's mother lives by herself on the next ranch. Janie's begged her to move here, but she says there's too many of us already." He paused, but Sam didn't say anything. "Janie wanted to hire somebody to stay with her, help with the housework and keep an eye on her. She refuses to have a stranger in her house."

When he paused again Janie entered the conversation. "Sam, I'm so worried about her. Sometimes she gets a little forgetful about turning off the stove and things. I'm her only child. But I don't want to live apart from Pete."

"Grandma is getting that bad?" Rich asked, studying his parents.

"She's seventy-five, Rich. You forget that because you don't see her that often," Janie assured him.

"Look," Pete began, looking at Samantha. "I know you said you needed a job. This is a perfect job. You could live there with room and board paid for five hundred dollars a week. And it would mean so much to Janie."

"But—but," Sam began, "you said she wouldn't let a stranger move in. I've never met her."

"No," Janie agreed, "but she thinks she knows you. I talked to her about you when we were trying to adopt you. And I lied to her. I told her you were overwhelmed by the size of the Randall crew. I told her she could take care of you.'' She held up her hand as Samantha started to protest. ''I know you don't need anyone to take care of you, but Mom's very sensitive about her age. She has her pride, you know.''

''I'd be glad to help you out, but I couldn't take money just for staying with her. And I need to be in town for a job.''

''That's the beauty of this plan, Sam,'' Pete said. ''Your job is right there. Will you try it for a week? You might not think we'd be paying you enough at the end of the week. Rich said you don't really have a job picked out yet. Couldn't you try it out for just a week?''

''Pete, I don't think—'' She stared into their anxious gazes. Finally she said, ''Okay, just for a week.''

''Samantha, you're an angel. If, after a week, you think Lavinia is too difficult, we'll take you to town,'' Pete said with a warm smile.

Janie was ecstatic. ''I can't tell you how much this means to me, Samantha. It's just like you really are my daughter!''

Pete was afraid his darling wife had gotten too carried away. Samantha seemed embarrassed by Janie's enthusiasm, so he added, ''If you don't mind, we'll take you over when we finish eating, and introduce you to Lavinia.''

Rich had watched the entire scheme play out, a strange expression on his face. Now he said, ''I'll go with you so I can see Grandma. I should have called her last night.''

"Good, dear," Janie said and took another bite of her sandwich.

RICH WASN'T SURE what was going on. He hadn't realized his grandmother was losing her sharpness. This was something he'd like to discuss with Russ, but his twin was in Rawhide working in the accounting office, and Rich would rather go with his parents and Samantha than into town.

His father was driving his truck with the double cab to accommodate all of them. Janie insisted on joining Samantha in the back seat since Rich needed to stretch out his leg.

"How are you feeling, son?" Pete asked as he got behind the wheel. "Have you taken a pain pill today?"

"Nope. If I did, I'd be sleeping right now. Those things are potent!"

"Yeah, I was worried when Sam said you had three the first day."

Rich cast a look over his shoulder at Sam before he answered his father. "I think Sam gave them to me so I wouldn't expect her to make conversation."

"I gave them to you because you were in pain," she said calmly, not getting upset about his taunt.

"But you liked not having to talk to me."

"Lose all your charm while you were in the rodeo?" Pete teased his son.

"Well, those bulls of yours weren't too impressed. It was Dynamite that caused all my problems."

"But you stayed on him, didn't you?" Pete asked, pride in his voice.

Janie, from the back seat, said, "That's disgusting, Pete. You're proud of him for breaking his ankle."

"Nope. But I'm proud of him for going the distance. He came in second."

Janie rolled her eyes at Sam. "Men!"

Samantha chuckled, and Rich stared at her. He hadn't seen such a pretty smile from her before.

She looked at him. "What?"

"You look pretty when you smile."

She immediately froze. "I've smiled before."

Rich nodded, but he added, "Not nearly enough."

She stared out the side window, her features frozen, and Rich realized he'd embarrassed her. In an effort to put her at ease, he said, "If you want to get on Grandma's good side, get her to teach you how to knit. She tried to teach me and Russ when we were little."

"You should have seen the miserable pieces of wool they turned out. Both of them had what was supposed to be a square, but I've never seen a square with five sides," Janie said with a grin.

Samantha chuckled again.

Rich, becoming addicted to that rich sound, added, "Grandma said we were clumsy and unmotivated. So we moved on to cooking. With the reward of eating the cookies we made, we became expert bakers," he bragged.

"Mom's a great cook," Janie agreed.

Samantha frowned, staring at Janie. "Still? I mean she still cooks well?"

"Oh, yes. When we go over for Sunday dinner, she's

always cooked enough for a month. She misses cooking for Daddy. She'll enjoy having you there to cook for.''

"But I thought she needed someone to take care of her.''

Pete hurriedly said, "She needs company more than anything. Someone to talk to. It's only occasionally that she forgets things.'' He cast a warning look over his shoulder to his wife.

"Here we are,'' Rich added. "Mom's parents have always been our closest neighbors. Russ and I would ride over on our ponies to visit.''

SAMANTHA WAS BEGINNING to wonder if she'd been set up. However, she did believe the part about Lavinia being lonely was most likely true. When a person got used to having someone around, it would be hard when their companion died. She decided to go ahead and stay out the week. For Pete and Janie's sakes.

By the time Pete had stopped the truck, an older woman was out on the porch. She looked a lot like Janie, and not nearly old enough to be seventy-five.

Rich hobbled out of the truck. "Grandma!'' he called, so Samantha had no doubt who she was. She watched Rich hug his grandmother, pleasure all over him. How nice to have generations of your family to enjoy.

Pete helped her out of the back and escorted her to the older woman. "Lavinia, this is Samantha.''

Lavinia left Rich's hug to stare at her guest.

Samantha had butterflies in her stomach. The woman

didn't know her. She might refuse to let Sam stay. It worried Samantha that it mattered so much to her.

A smile broke across Lavinia's face. ''Welcome, my almost-granddaughter. I'm glad you've come.''

Samantha blinked her tears away and stepped forward to shake hands. Instead, Lavinia swept her into her arms.

Samantha was overwhelmed by the woman's gesture of warmth.

''Come on in,'' Lavinia said, and hurried her into the house. ''I made chocolate pie when I heard you were coming. Rich, honey, can you get the plates and forks? Oh, I shouldn't have asked you with your hurt ankle.''

''No problem, Grandma. I can do it.''

Samantha watched Rich obey his grandmother, a funny smile on her lips. The autocratic man she'd met in Flagstaff was completely different around his mother and grandmother.

Once they were all seated and eating the delicious pie, Lavinia plied Samantha with questions.

''Why did you decide to leave Flagstaff?''

Sam chewed on her bottom lip, undecided about how much to tell them. But Rich left her no choice.

''Tell them about Brad.''

''Who's Brad?'' Pete asked.

''Her boss.'' Rich stared at her, waiting.

''He wasn't a nice man. I thought I'd be better off getting away from him,'' Sam said, keeping her voice even.

Again Rich pushed her. ''His wife died suspiciously a month ago. He wanted Sam to be his fifth.''

"Is that true, Sam?" Pete asked sharply. "Did he hurt you?"

"No, of course not. He's back in Flagstaff and I can tell you that's a long drive away." She smiled, then turned to Rich. "How's Bella? Did she stand the trip okay?"

"Sure. She's used to moving around."

Lavinia jumped in with another question about Sam's father and mother. Those were easier questions to answer. It had been a long time since her father died and she didn't have any fond remembrances of him. She couldn't remember her mother at all since she'd died in childbirth.

When there was a break in the conversation, Samantha stood up and began carrying their dishes to the sink. She noticed the kitchen was sparkling clean. There weren't even any dirty dishes from baking the pie.

"Here, child," Lavinia protested, "I can clean up."

"No need. If you're willing to take me in, I'll do the cleanup."

Rich got to his feet. "I can help, Grandma."

"You should rest your ankle," Samantha protested.

"I've been resting it all morning. You wash, I'll dry."

"Dictatorial as usual," she muttered, hoping the others couldn't hear.

"Okay, I'll wash and you dry."

"How about I wash and dry and you rest your ankle?"

Samantha heard a laugh and she looked at the three at the table.

Lavinia asked, "Do you two always argue? It reminds me of Janie and Pete."

Rich protested. "Mom and Dad? They don't argue much."

"Maybe not now, but they argued up a storm before they got married. Had the men in both families upset because the women wouldn't speak to them, made them sleep on the sofas."

"Why?" Rich asked.

"Because I said she should marry me since she was pregnant. And I was right." Pete smiled triumphantly at his wife.

"I think I won, Pete," Janie said. "I didn't want to unless you loved me. And you do."

"With all my heart, honey. But that wasn't ever in question."

Both Lavinia and Janie laughed. "But you wouldn't tell me," Janie pointed out.

Pete was beginning to look a little uncomfortable. "No need to discuss it further. Since we've been married more than twenty-five years and had three kids, I think everyone knows we're a great match."

Though Janie chuckled, she stood and held out her hand. "Let's take Sam's bag upstairs. Is everything ready, Mom?"

"Sure." Lavinia looked at Rich and Sam at the sink. "You two come up when you're finished."

When they were alone in the kitchen, Samantha said, "Do you think your grandmother needs someone to take care of her?"

Rich gave her a sharp look, then concentrated on the

saucer he was drying. "I think she gets very lonely with Granddad gone. He was a crusty old guy. But she adored him."

"Yes."

"I'm glad you're staying. I want Grandma to be happy."

"I've only promised to stay a week."

"You might like it. I don't think you'll be too lonely with Grandma here. And the ranch hands will probably be happy to spend time with you." By the time he finished speaking, he was frowning deeply.

"Is there something wrong with that?"

"No, but, well, cowboys talk a lot but they don't always keep their promises. I don't want you to get hurt."

"I told you I could take care of myself, Rich."

"Yeah, but I don't want that, either. I want you to be happy, too."

She put the last clean saucer in the dish rack and let the water drain from the sink. "Your grandmother doesn't have a dishwasher?"

"Didn't want one. Dad tried to talk her into a kitchen renovation with all the latest gadgets ten years ago. She refused."

"Are you coming up?" Lavinia's voice floated down the stairs.

"On our way!" Rich sang out.

He took Sam's hand and led her up the stairs. She tried to pull away when they reached the top of the stairs, but he held on. "Are you in Mom's room?" he called.

"Yes," Lavinia answered. "But now it will be Samantha's room."

Samantha stepped into the room where Janie, Lavinia and Pete were waiting. She stared at the beautiful room and fought back the tears.

Chapter Seven

Three days with Lavinia and Samantha knew sh
in trouble. Her self-discipline had eroded to the
that she knew she'd never want to voluntarily
Lavinia treated her like a favorite child. She was
ful and loving. Sam had never experienced such
vironment.

She rose when the alarm went off. She'd alway
an early riser, though she didn't normally rise
thirty. But Lavinia did. She insisted on cooking
fast each morning, but Sam set the table and c
up afterward.

She'd persuaded Lavinia to let her do the vacu
and clean the bathrooms, too, but it had taken a
mined argument. Those chores took at most an h
two each day. Sam fixed lunch and the two o
made dinner together, but Sam enjoyed those tas
pecially since there was an abundance of food ar
the two of them to eat.

Sam figured she was going to gain weight
wasn't careful.

She came downstairs this morning, a smile

lips. She had nothing to frown about. "Morning, Lavinia," she called as she entered the kitchen.

"Good morning, dear. I do enjoy having you here. I really was feeling lonely."

"I'm lucky to be here. But I don't feel I'm earning my keep."

"Nonsense. I'm making pancakes this morning."

"I'm going to have to watch my weight. You're such a good cook, Lavinia."

"You're not bad yourself, Samantha. You'll make some man a fine wife."

Sam stopped in her tracks. "I don't think so. I'm not interested in marrying."

Lavinia turned around. "Why's that?"

"Men like me, but not for the role of wife. I have no family, nothing of value. They see me as just a short-term fling, but I'm not interested in that role."

"I should think not! And if Rich, or any of the boys, act like that, you let me know. I won't put up with that kind of behavior."

Sam smiled. "Don't worry, Lavinia. I can take care of myself."

After breakfast, Lavinia offered to show Samantha how to knit. Sam had told her last night that she'd like to learn how. They settled in the comfy den and Lavinia pulled out several skeins of green wool. Sam learned quickly. Lavinia watched her, a smile on her lips.

A knock at the door surprised both ladies. "I'll get it," Lavinia said, "so you won't drop any stitches."

Sam figured it would be someone for Lavinia anyway, since she didn't know anyone but the Randalls.

She didn't figure Rich, Janie or Pete would knock on the back door.

Lavinia came back into the room, a worried look on her face. Samantha was worried, too, when she saw who followed Lavinia.

"Brad! What are you doing here?"

"Like I told Mrs. Dawson, I'm here to take you home. You shouldn't have run so far just because we had a little argument."

"How did you find me?"

"One of your boyfriend's friends came back in. He told me Randall's name and I checked the rodeo files for his address. Once I got to Rawhide, it only took one visit to a café to find out where you were. People like to talk."

Sam kept her gaze on Brad. She knew he was mean, and had a bad temper. She was worried about Lavinia standing so close to him. All she wanted to do was make sure he left. Quickly. "I think you misunderstood, Brad. I was tired of Flagstaff. I didn't want to stay there."

"You'll change your mind," he said in an arrogant tone.

Sam turned to Lavinia, and said "I'd better step out on the porch and talk to Brad."

"Of course, dear. I'm sure your young man would like to visit alone. You've certainly come a long way, haven't you?" she asked Brad.

"She's worth it," Brad said. As if he were a gentleman, he stepped back and waved Samantha in front of him.

Once they stepped outside, she turned to face him. "I don't know why you're here, but I want nothing to do with you."

"Yes, you do," he said, confidence in his voice. "I know you're all alone. No one will care if I take you back to Arizona." He flashed her an evil grin.

He grabbed her arm and started pulling her toward his truck.

"*I* object, even if no one else will," she said. This wasn't the first time Sam had faced a bully, planning on using his strength to take what he wanted. She'd actually taken a self-defense course for just such occasions.

He had her off the porch, dragging her to the truck. She still thought maybe she could convince him to leave her alone, until he drew a big knife as he grew more irritated with her resistance. She knew she had to do something now.

Suddenly, she dropped as if she'd fainted.

Brad growled and yanked on her arm, causing her a lot of pain, but she didn't give in. He leaned over to force her to her feet. Samantha raised a leg and kicked him in the groin as hard as she could. He folded over in pain and she kicked him in the face. He released her as he screamed in rage. She rolled to the side so he wouldn't fall on her.

Then she grabbed the rocking chair on the porch and slammed the hard wood down on his head and he slumped flat on the ground.

"Good girl," Lavinia said, stepping out of the house

with a rifle in her hands. "You did that slick as a⁣
tle. But you're bleeding. What happened?"

Sam looked down at her arm, shocked to di⁣
he'd cut her arm as he fell. She grabbed the ⁣
knowing she had to stop the bleeding.

"We'd better get out of here. He's going to b⁣
ous when he comes to. I'll drive you to Janie's⁣
and we can call the sheriff to pick him up. Then⁣
on my way." She hated the fact that her voice tre⁣

Lavinia ignored her. "I'll get a towel." She ⁣
back inside and reappeared with a clean soft clo⁣
think you're going to have some bruises on you⁣
too."

"Didn't you hear me, Lavinia? We need to—⁣

"I heard you, child. But I've already called th⁣
iff." She paused when they both heard a vehicle ⁣
down the long driveway. "That will be Rich. Th⁣
iff couldn't get here so quickly."

"You called Rich? But he's injured. I don'⁣
anything else to happen to him on my behalf."

Lavinia grinned. "Don't worry. Rich can't⁣
Brad now 'cause you already did."

The truck came over the hill and the driver ⁣
slam on his brakes until the last minute. The ⁣
opened and Rich, Red and a young man Samant⁣
only seen once, Toby Randall, raced to the front⁣
They all stopped when they saw Brad lying ⁣
ground.

"Is he alive?" Rich wanted to know.

"I hope so. I didn't mean to kill him," Sa⁣
said, taking a hesitant step toward the body.

"I'll check," Toby said, kneeling beside him.

Rich stared at her. "What happened to your arm?"

"He had a knife," Sam said, but she was beginning to weaken as she bled and the adrenaline faded.

Toby picked up the knife that had fallen near the man. "Here it is."

"How'd he find you?" Rich asked. "You didn't call the café, did you?"

"Of course not!" Samantha snapped, irritated that Rich thought she'd do something so stupid.

"Then how would he know?" Rich asked again.

"One of your friends came into the restaurant and he asked your name. He checked the rodeo records. Once he got to town, gossip did the rest. He was determined to take me back."

"What? Grandma, are you okay?"

"I'm fine, Rich. It's Samantha who got hurt. Look at that cut on her arm. She's going to need stitches."

Samantha tried to hide her right arm behind her back, but Rich stepped to her side and gently pulled it forward, unwrapping the towel.

Red whistled. "That looks painful."

Samantha stared at the blood still seeping through the cut. "It's almost stopped bleeding." It was painful, but she said nothing else.

The sound of a siren caught their attention. At the same time, Brad stirred.

Samantha took a step back and she warned Toby to get away from him. "He's crazy."

"We can tell that," he assured her. "We don't much cotton to men who threaten defenseless women."

"Defenseless? Take another look, Toby Randa[ll]
Lavinia ordered. "Samantha weighs about a hal[f]
what that man does and she took care of him. And [I]
got my rifle in case he tries anything else. We're [not]
defenseless."

"You're right, Mrs. Dawson. I'm sure this guy [will]
agree with you, too," Toby said, grinning.

The sheriff's car pulled up and two men got out. [The]
older one called, "Mrs. Dawson? Are you all right[?]"

"I'm fine. But he's not."

The sheriff and his deputy stepped into the ci[rcle,]
able to see the man for the first time. "I can see [he's]
been taken out. Now, Toby, Rich, I hope you di[dn't]
overdo it. We don't want him bringing assault cha[rges]
against you."

Rich grinned. "We wish we were the ones to [take]
him down. Especially after he did this." He ge[ntly]
pulled Samantha's arm forward again. "But it was S[am]
herself who took care of the guy."

The deputy's jaw dropped and the sheriff looke[d at]
Samantha in admiration. "I see. I can call an am[bu]-
lance."

"No, thank you, Sheriff. I'm fine," Sam replied.

"We'll drive her to Doc's now. We can fill yo[u in]
later, okay? I think she'd better get stitches right awa[y,]"
Rich assured the sheriff.

"Good idea. Bob," the sheriff said. "Put some c[uffs]
on this guy and put him in the back of the car. T[hen]
we'll stop blocking their way out of here."

The deputy tried to pull Brad to his feet, but he [was]
too heavy. Toby offered a hand. The deputy turned B[rad]

around and started to cuff him. Brad yanked his arm away and tried to hit the deputy, roaring, "You have nothing on me. Don't touch me."

The sheriff didn't hesitate. He pulled a pistol and leveled it at Brad's head. "You're under arrest. If you resist, I'll shoot you. Got that?"

"You can't do that!" Brad insisted and took a step toward the sheriff.

The sheriff pulled back the hammer on his gun. "Try me."

Samantha didn't figure the sheriff got many takers on that offer. His voice sounded made of steel. Brad hesitated.

"Now, put your hands behind your back and let my deputy cuff you."

"I want to file assault charges!" Brad roared, but he actually did as the sheriff ordered.

"Against whom?" the sheriff asked calmly.

"That woman, damn her! She tried to hurt me on purpose."

"You'll get a chance to talk to a lawyer as soon as we get you to jail. But it'll be hard to convince a jury that this little lady brought you down for no reason," he added with a grin. Then he turned to Samantha and Lavinia. "Are you taking your car, Lavinia? I'll help this lady to the car."

Rich shook his head. "I'm taking them in. That is, Grandma will have to drive, but I'm going with them. Come on, Sam." He put an arm around her waist and urged her forward.

She leaned toward him. "I can slap on a Band-Aid. I don't need to see the doctor."

"You're going to the doctor, Sam. That's a deep cut. It'll probably leave a scar but it's got to be cleaned out and sewn up."

Samantha tried to resist, but her head was hurting, her arm throbbing, and she thought she'd done something to her collarbone. She didn't have much strength left. By the time he got her to the car, slipping both of them into the back seat, Lavinia was behind the wheel.

"We'll see you in town," the sheriff said and got in the police car. The driver turned the sedan around and sped down the driveway.

Rich didn't have to tell his grandmother to hurry. She was on their tail in no time.

RICH CARRIED Sam into the doctor's office even though she insisted she could walk. Rich didn't believe her, which was probably a good thing.

"Where's Doc Jacoby?" he asked as he walked past the patients waiting in reception.

The young lady behind a small desk looked up. "What's wrong?"

Rich pressed his lips tightly together, trying to control his anger. Then he repeated, "Where's Doc Jacoby? We've got an emergency!"

"What's up, boy?" asked an elderly man who had just come through an open door near the reception desk.

"Doc, this is Samantha Jeffers. Her arm has been cut and she's lost a lot of blood. You need to take a look

at her.'' Rich turned so the doctor could see Sam's right
arm.

Dr. Jacoby had been taking care of him and his family most of their lives. Rich trusted him completely.

''Nasty cut. How did that happen?'' Dr. Jacoby
asked.

''Some guy took a knife to her. Can you take care
of her?''

Doc turned to his other patients. ''Sorry, folks, but I
have to attend to this young lady right now.''

He ushered them into an examination room and
turned to Sam.

''So, can you talk, young lady?''

''Yes, of course. I really don't think there's anything
you can do, but Rich insisted—''

''You a friend of Rich?'' Doc asked, looking first at
her and then Rich.

Lavinia, entering the room behind them, spoke up.
''No, she's my companion.''

Doc sent a sharp look Lavinia's way. ''You okay,
Lavinia? Didn't know you had a companion.'' He
shouted for a nurse. When a woman appeared in
starched white, he asked her to help the patient put on
a gown.

''Please, Doctor,'' Sam began, ''I don't need—''

Both Rich and Lavinia assured her Doc Jacoby was
the best. She needed to follow his orders.

The nurse indicated for Rich to set Sam down on the
examining table and turned to pull a disposable gown
out of a drawer.

''Rich,'' Lavinia caught his attention. ''You need to

leave so we can undress Sam. We don't want any m
blood on her clothes.''

He turned bright red and stepped to the door. ''D
let her fall,'' he said before closing the door behind h

''Your grandson seems mighty intent on this li
patient,'' the nurse said, grinning at Lavinia.

''He surely does,'' Lavinia agreed with a big grin
her face.

''He just feels responsible for me,'' Samantha sa

Lavinia patted Sam's good arm, smiling gently at
and the nurse began unbuttoning Samantha's shirt.

''Really, I don't need to undress. It's already stop
bleeding. Maybe just a bandage?''

''You're being ridiculous, child,'' Lavinia protes
''Who knows where that knife has been. The cut ha
be cleaned and you'll get a tetanus shot. You'll n
stitches, too.''

The nurse held the injured arm, staring at it. ''W
is this skin all red?''

''It'll be black and blue real soon, I expect,'' Lavi
said. ''The guy who attacked her was pulling her
she was resisting. I bet he bruised it.''

''You can leave on your bra and jeans, dear. Just
this gown over them and we'll be ready.''

Samantha didn't feel she had any choice. After sh
put on the gown, the nurse opened the door for
doctor.

When Doctor Jacoby came back in, it was clear h
been talking to Rich. ''I hear you're new to Rawhid

''Yes,'' she said, glaring at Rich, who followed I
into the room.

"Now, don't blame the boy for that. I know everyone in town. Haven't seen you before."

She ducked her head.

"This man that hurt you. He got a beef with you?"

"He wanted me to be his fifth wife," Sam said in disgust.

"His fifth? What happened to the others?"

"The police are looking into that."

"Mercy, I hope they keep him locked up. Doesn't sound like someone we want here in Rawhide." He picked up her arm and looked at the cut again. "I'm going to have to clean this up. It may sting a little, so Nurse Banning is going to give you a local to ease the pain. Once it's clean, we'll stitch it up and give you a tetanus shot as well. Probably eight stitches. Okay?"

Samantha lay still, staring at the ceiling as the nurse gave her a shot just above the cut. She couldn't believe she would need that many stitches, but she was feeling a little dizzy. It was easier to let him get on with it.

A few minutes later, the doctor assured her they were all done with the stitching. "Now then, your arm is all red. Looks like a pretty bad bruise."

Samantha only nodded.

"Do you hurt anywhere else?"

She tried to move her cut arm, but the nurse stopped her and asked, "Can you use your other arm, dear?"

Samantha used her other arm and touched her shoulder on the injured side. She thought she'd pulled a muscle.

"Ah," the doctor said. "I think we'd better do an X ray. We don't want to miss anything."

"Something else is wrong?" Rich demanded, stepping into Sam's line of vision.

"Won't know until we look. You and Lavinia are going to have to wait outside."

"Why can't we stay?" Rich demanded, a frown on his face.

"Because we're going to do an X ray. Go sit down and we'll let you know when we're done."

Samantha watched Rich and Lavinia leave with a sense of loss. For a young woman who had always been alone, she'd quickly come to appreciate their company.

The nurse told Sam to remain on the table. Then she left the room only to return right away with a big machine she could just barely get through the door. Then she handed the doctor a lead apron and put one on herself.

"How's the pain?" the doctor asked as the nurse slid an X-ray plate under her right side.

"Bearable," Sam told him as she gritted her teeth.

"You're braver than some of these cowboys around here," he assured her with a chuckle. "By the way, I noticed Rich has a cast on his foot. How come?"

"He fell wrong from the back of a bull."

"Where?"

"Flagstaff," she replied, grimacing at the nurse's movement.

"Okay, we're almost ready," the doctor said. "When I tell you, hold your breath."

Chapter Eight

Rich immediately began to pace in the waiting room. Lavinia took a seat and chatted with her neighbors, explaining what had happened.

Suddenly the door flew open and Janie, closely followed by Red, entered the room.

"Rich? Where is she? Is she all right?"

He hugged his mother. "Doc sewed up the cut, but he's doing an X ray now."

"Why? What else is wrong? And who is this man? Why would he attack Samantha?"

Lavinia moved down the sofa and patted the seat she'd abandoned. "Sit down, Janie. We'll tell you what we know." She waited until Janie had done so. "The man said his name was Brad. Apparently Sam used to work for him. And he wanted her to go back to Arizona."

"And she agreed?" Janie asked, her voice rising.

"No. He was trying to force her." Lavinia pressed her hands together. "That's when I ran to get my rifle. When I got back, he was knocked on the ground. That's when I saw Sam was bleeding. I got a towel to stop the bleeding. Then Rich arrived and we brought Sam in. The sheriff took that Brad fellow into custody.''

''What I don't get is how he knew where she was,'' Rich said, anger in his voice.

''She said she didn't tell him,'' Lavinia replied. ''Said she knew he was dangerous.''

''The important thing is she's going to be all right, isn't she?'' Janie asked. ''I told Toby to tell your dad.''

As if on cue, the phone on the receptionist's desk rang. She answered it, then looked at Janie. ''Ma'am, your husband wants to talk to you.''

By the time Janie finished her conversation with Pete, the nurse was waiting to take them to the doctor's office.

All three of them asked questions nonstop. The nurse opened the doctor's office door and asked them to be seated. ''The doctor will be here in a minute to fill you all in.'' Then she disappeared.

Fortunately, Dr. Jacoby entered just then, his hand raised. ''My nurse warned me you were all demanding answers. Samantha lost quite a bit of blood, and she's turning black and blue on her arm and shoulder. The man wrenched her shoulder. It will be okay but it's painful. She's being taken to a room and we're keeping her overnight at least. Maybe two nights.'' After a pause, he said, ''And that's all I know, except she is a strong woman. Suffered a lot of pain without complaining.''

''Can we see her?'' Janie asked.

''In about two hours. After they settle her in, they're

going to give her some pain medication that will knock her out. When she wakes up, she'll feel a lot better.''

"Okay, thanks, Doc," Janie said, and led her son and mother out to the waiting room where Red was waiting.

ONCE THEY LEFT the clinic, Rich glowered. "I think I'm paying the sheriff a visit."

"Is he going to charge the man with anything?" Janie asked.

"He'd better," Rich returned.

"I think we should go get Samantha her own things," Lavinia said. "I remember that made me feel lots better when I was in the hospital."

"After we stop at the sheriff's office," Rich replied.

"All right, dear."

"While y'all do that, Red and I are going home to reassure Mildred and pick up Pete. He'll want to see Sam, too."

Rich got in his grandmother's car on the passenger side, irritated that he had to rely on anyone to drive him wherever he needed to go.

Lavinia pulled up beside the sheriff's office but stayed in the car. "I'm beginning to feel a little sore and tired," she admitted. "I'll just wait here until you're ready to go home."

"You sure you're all right, Grandma?"

"I'm sure. Maybe I'm just hungry. It's past lunch-time."

"I won't be long."

When Rich walked in, he discovered the sheriff talking to one of his deputies. "Sheriff Metzger?" he called.

The sheriff spun on his heels. "Rich. How's your friend?"

"Doc's keeping her overnight."

"I'm sorry. Her attacker is going back to Flagstaff first thing in the morning. He wasn't supposed to leave town. They've got new evidence on his last wife's death. Looks like they're going to charge him with her murder and look into his other wives' deaths, so your little lady won't have to worry about him."

"That's good news, but she's just a friend, not my lady."

"Uh, right."

"So does Sam need to file charges just in case he beats that rap?"

"That would be best."

"If you'll give me the forms she needs to sign, I'll bring them by later."

The sheriff gathered up several sheets of paper and handed them to Rich. After saying goodbye, Rich hurried back to his grandmother's car.

"You want to get some lunch before we go back to the ranch?" he asked her.

"No, we'll grab something to eat when we get home. I want to get Samantha's nightgown and grooming things to her as quick as possible. I was right glad to get out of that thing they called a nightgown when I was in the hospital."

Rich nodded, but he wondered what Sam would have

in the way of a nightgown. Then he shook his head. That wasn't a good thing for him to worry about.

When they returned to his grandmother's house, she ordered him to get the ham out of the refrigerator. They'd have sandwiches. He did as she asked, taking out mustard and bread as well.

His grandmother then went upstairs to Samantha's bedroom. A few minutes later, she came back down with Samantha's duffel bag. "Did you say this was the only bag she brought?" she asked.

"Yeah."

"There's no nightgown in her room. Just a couple of T-shirts and a spare pair of jeans."

"I figured."

"Well, why didn't you say something? We could've gone to a store."

Rich shook his head. "Sam's real independent, Grandma. I'm not sure but what buying her something will upset her."

"Mercy!" Lavinia exclaimed. She picked up the phone to call her daughter. "Janie, Samantha doesn't have hardly anything. There's no nightgown and Rich says buying her something will upset her. What do we do?"

After listening, Lavinia hung up the phone and started making sandwiches.

"What did Mom say?" Rich asked, frowning.

"She said she and Pete would talk to Samantha. We're each going to buy her a nightgown, so she'll have more than one, but we'll keep them simple. How many sandwiches do you want?'' she asked, switching the subject.

''One,'' he said, absentmindedly.

''One? You usually have two at least,'' Lavinia pointed out.

''I'm not getting a lot of exercise with this cast on my foot. What should *I* get her?''

''Well, I don't think it would be proper for you to get her a nightie,'' Lavinia assured him with a grin.

''Of course not! I didn't mean— I wasn't thinking of that. But if you all are taking her presents, I don't want to show up empty-handed,'' he explained in irritation.

He had no intention of getting intimate with Samantha. Unlike Russ, he wasn't ready to marry. But Samantha was a friend. He'd brought her here. And it was normal to get a little warm thinking about a woman's nightclothes. It didn't mean anything.

''Maybe your mother will think of something,'' Lavinia said, fixing the sandwiches.

Rich poured two glasses of iced tea. ''When is she coming over?''

''As soon as your dad comes in.''

Rich frowned again. ''Dad doesn't come in until almost dark. I thought we should take Sam her things now.''

''Don't worry. He's coming in early.''

Rich stood there, his hands on his hips. Did his father really think of Samantha as a daughter? Rich certainly didn't think of her as a sister. In fact, he realized now that he'd been attracted to her from the beginning. On the drive up, the more she pushed him away, the more he'd wanted to know about her. He'd visited a couple of times since she'd moved to his grandmother's, but Sam hadn't shown any delight upon his arrival. If anything, she'd withdrawn again.

"Sit and eat, boy. They'll be here in half an hour," Lavinia ordered, a smile on her lips.

THE DOCTOR HAD instructed the nurses to give Samantha painkillers after they got her in bed. As the medicine took effect and she slid into sleep, she vaguely heard voices talking by the bed.

"Who is she? Doc said she's a friend of Rich Randall."

"Maybe some woman's finally caught him. She's pretty enough. And I heard she took down a big man, so maybe she took Rich down, too. In a different way," the voice added with a chuckle.

Samantha tried to speak, but her tongue seemed thick. She tried again, but finally gave up, losing consciousness.

When she awoke several hours later, it wasn't just her tongue that didn't operate. Her mind seemed blank, too.

"Samantha?"

She struggled to open her eyes and discovered Dr. Jacoby by her bed, taking her pulse. "Hi," she whispered. "Throat dry."

"Nurse, get her some water," the doctor ordered and the woman came into Sam's line of vision with a glass with a bendable straw in it.

Samantha sipped the water slowly.

"I believe you have some visitors waiting," th
tor said cheerfully.

Samantha frowned. "No. No visitors."

"You don't feel up to visitors?"

"No. There's no one to visit."

"You're wrong there, young lady," he said
departing.

"Shall I raise the head of your bed a little?
make it easier to visit." Without waiting for an ar
the nurse pushed a button, elevating Samantha's

Almost simultaneously, the door opened agai
Lavinia and Rich, accompanied by Pete and Janie,
into the room.

Pete reached the bed and leaned over to ki
cheek. "Hi, honey. Sorry you had such a hard
How are you feeling?"

"Pete," she managed to say, suddenly fighting

Janie replaced him and kissed her cheek, too.
dear. I'm sorry it took us so long to bring your
to you. Did you sleep some?"

"Yes," Sam replied. "You didn't have to con

"Do you think I'm going to let my handsome
band visit a beautiful woman and me not come?
there'd be rumors all over town." Janie's big gri
Sam she didn't mean it. At least she hoped so.

Lavinia stepped forward. "Did Doc give you
medicine?"

"Something to help me sleep. Pete, can you t
him? He wants me to stay overnight." Alarm ha
voice rising.

"What's the matter, Sam? You got a heavy da

morrow?'' Pete asked grinning. "I think you'd best do what Doc says.''

Almost as if he felt he was being ignored, Rich came to the other side of her bed and picked up her left hand. "Did he say why?''

"No. He said we'd talk about it later.'' She looked at Rich hopefully. "I can take care of myself. I won't cause Lavinia any trouble, I promise. I think she'll let me stay at her house until I'm feeling better.'' Her gaze shifted to Lavinia to see if she objected to that remark.

Janie and Pete exchanged a look that she couldn't interpret. Then Pete said, "Honey, I told you, you belong with us. No one is sending you away. We're going to take care of you. You're one of us, now.''

"I can't stay, Pete. I put Lavinia in danger. I can't promise it won't happen again. Brad is mean and vicious.''

"If anything does happen, it won't be Brad causing trouble,'' Rich assured her. "They're charging him with the murder of his fourth wife. And maybe for the others, too. He's going to be put away for a long time.''

"Besides, we did a good job of protecting ourselves, young lady. We're the talk of the town.'' Lavinia beamed at her, as if that were a desirable thing. "Now, open this.''

She thrust a box at Samantha that she hadn't noticed before.

Samantha stared at the box. "I—I can't— What is it?''

"That's why you're supposed to open it, silly,'' Lavinia teased her.

Her gaze flashed to both Pete and Janie, then Rich. "I can't."

"Rich, you help her," Janie ordered.

He put something on the floor and stepped to her bedside, lifting the lid off Lavinia's box. Inside, nestled in tissue paper, was a pale-green short nightgown, along with a matching robe. Rich lifted the two garments out of the box, putting them across the cover so she could see them.

"No! No, I can't. Lavinia—"

Janie stopped her. "I know you're independent, but, Sam, we'd do the same thing for anyone else. If you don't want them when you leave, you can just leave them behind. But we want you to have them."

Sam looked even more alarmed. "Them? There's more?"

"You'll need a change, especially if you stay another night," Janie explained. "Besides, do you know how long I've waited to have a daughter to shop for? You'll be doing me a favor."

Rich reached out for the next box and opened it, too. Inside was a white gown and robe. It, too, was simple, but it had lace edging the neckline and armholes.

Sam reached out and stroked the soft material of both gowns. She'd never had anything as nice. "You're all so sweet. I—I don't know how I'll repay you."

"We'll tell you when our birthdays are coming up. And we'll expect good presents," Pete told her, grinning.

"Now, you men scoot out so we can make Sam comfortable," Janie ordered. The men quickly departed.

"She lives with me, so I say she wears the green one first," Lavinia insisted.

"Of course, Mom," Janie said, "if that's okay with Samantha." She looked at her and Sam nodded. "Okay, lean forward just a little bit and I'll untie the one you're wearing. I hate those ties."

When she pulled the hospital gown away, she immediately slipped the pale-green gown onto Sam's head. Then, very gently, she put Samantha's injured arm through the armhole. "We picked out gowns with big armholes, so it would be easier."

Lavinia, on the other side of the bed, held the gown for Sam to put her uninjured arm in. Then she smoothed it down over Sam's body and drew the cover up over her. "The green looks good. Makes those huge eyes of yours look even bigger." Then she looked at her daughter, grinning, "Do you think it's safe to let Rich see her like this?"

Something in what she said reminded Samantha of that conversation she'd overheard as she drifted into sleep. She frowned, trying to remember what had bothered her.

"You don't like it?" Lavinia asked.

Samantha saw the concern on Lavinia's face and she immediately reassured her. "I love it. It feels so silky and cool. Thank you, Lavinia. It's wonderful of you, and you and Pete, too, Janie, to bring me these things. I was just trying to remember something that was bothering me. That's why I frowned."

"Rich brought you something, too," Lavinia assured her. She turned away from the bed and picked up a small blue, woven bag with flowers. "He thought you could use a bag for your new nightgowns. And he put in all your grooming things from your duffel bag."

Samantha turned bright red. "I—I don't have much."

"Don't worry about it," Janie assured her. Then she put the jeans and T-shirt she'd been wearing that morning into the case along with the white peignoir set. "I'd better invite the men back in before they get too antsy."

Rich and Pete must've been waiting right outside the door because they entered at once.

"You look pretty," Pete said immediately. "Feeling a little better?" he asked.

Sam dutifully answered, "Yes, of course." In truth, the pain was coming back.

"Okay, we're going to go have dinner, but we'll check with you later before we head for the house," Janie said. "Some of the others may be in to visit. Red and Mildred are definitely planning on it. But if you get tired, just shoo them away."

She and Lavinia and Pete each kissed Samantha's cheek and headed for the door. Pete looked over his shoulder. "You coming, Rich?"

"I'll be right there. I need to get her signature for the sheriff," he said. "Go ahead and get a table and I'll be there in five minutes."

Suddenly, Samantha was alone with Rich. She'd spent several days in the truck with him, but this was different. "What do I need to sign?" she asked hurriedly.

He pulled a folded sheet of paper out of his back

pocket. "This paper is to press assault charges against Brad."

"But I thought you said he was being charged with murder."

"He is, but we want to be sure he doesn't escape all the charges. Just sign on the bottom line. I filled out the rest of the information."

He offered a pen and then realized at the same time that she did that it was going to be impossible to write her name. At least by herself. "Damn, I didn't think of that. I'll talk to the sheriff tomorrow and ask if your signature can be postponed."

"Thank you. But I think I can do it if you'll support my arm." She wanted to be sure Brad wasn't let out of prison any time soon.

"Are you sure? We don't want to open up that cut."

"I'm sure the doctor's stitches will stay in place. Unless you don't want— I mean, I can do it by myself, probably. Give me the pen, please, and—"

Rich stepped closer to the bed, his features stiffening.

"I don't have rabies!" she snapped when he warily approached.

"I know that! I just don't want to hurt you," he added as he slid his hand under her injured arm. With his other hand, he slid the bed table over her lap and placed the form on it. "Okay, let's try it. But if it hurts too much, I'll talk to the sheriff about waiting."

Sam tried to hide how much effort it took to move the pen. However, she managed to produce a wobbly signature similar to her normal one. Then she lay back against the pillows and drew a deep breath, aware that Rich still held her arm. "Thank you."

He followed her gaze to her arm and eased his hold from her. "Good job. Did it hurt much?"

She shook her head. "Oh, and thank you for loaning me that bag. I appreciate it."

He looked at her for a long moment. "It isn't a loan, Sam. It's a gift."

"I—I—thank you."

He bent over, she supposed to kiss her cheek as his parents and grandmother had done. But Samantha wasn't prepared for that. She turned her head to tell him so, and his lips covered hers.

She'd been kissed before. When she was younger and wanted to know what all the excitement was about. And a few times when she wasn't willing but couldn't fight the man off. But none of those times had shown her the magic people talked about.

Her first thought was that Rich had made a mistake. But his lips had control of hers, and he didn't back away. Instead, his lips softened and gently urged her closer. The tip of his tongue stroked her mouth, teasing her. Then she realized how responsive she was. The last thought she had was she'd found heaven. But she couldn't! Panic rushed in.

With Rich, of all people, she found the magic of a kiss.

Chapter Nine

Pete kept an eye on the restaurant door, waiting for Rich's arrival. They'd left him at the hospital over a quarter hour ago and Pete couldn't help wonder what was taking him so long. But he wasn't into matchmaking, in spite of what Janie said.

He would like it if Rich fell for Samantha however, and brought her legally into the family. But only if Rich loved her. Pete knew his son's reputation as a love-'em-and-leave-'em kind of guy. After cautioning him to use condoms and be kind, he didn't figure there was much else he could do.

Rich came in, a scowl on his face.

Pete raised his hand. "Rich! Over here."

His son joined them at a table for six, barely greeting them as he sat. Then he buried his face in the menu.

Pete waited him out. When he finally came out from behind the menu, Pete asked, "Everything all right?"

"Yeah."

"I wondered because you took longer than we expected."

"Sorry, I ran into some friends and they wanted me

to tell them about Samantha. Why are we at such a big table?''

Janie smiled. ''Russ and Abby are joining us here. They hadn't heard about Sam's rough day.''

''Oh.''

The waitress arrived to take their orders. Janie also ordered for Rich's twin and his fiancée. After the waitress left, Rich asked, ''How do you know what they want?''

''They told me what they wanted on the phone. This way their food will arrive about the time they do. I think this new situation is working very well for Russ. He enjoys working with Bill Johnson in town and still doing some work at the ranch part-time,'' Janie enthused.

''More to the point, Dad and the uncles are behind him.'' Rich folded his arms across his chest and stared at his dad. He couldn't believe his twin enjoyed being a bean counter part-time. But, according to everyone, Russ was happy. He'd started working for the only accountant in town last fall, about the time Rich went off to the rodeo.

''It's working out all right,'' Pete replied. ''We hired an extra hand.''

Just then, several young men wandered by their table, stopping when they recognized Rich. ''Hey, Rich! Congratulations!''

''For what?'' Rich frowned.

''We heard you're getting married soon. To the new lady in town.''

Rich glared at the two men.

''That's what my girlfriend Beth said. She was working reception at the clinic when you brought that woman in. The news sure took us by surprise. We thought you wouldn't get caught so easily.''

"I'm not marrying anyone!" Rich snapped. "The lady's a friend and nothing else."

Their eyebrows raised. One of them said, "I heard she's good-looking. Green eyes and long, dark hair." He looked at Rich as if to confirm the rumor.

Rich stared at the table, ignoring them.

"'Fraid you got your facts wrong, boys. Rich is recovering from a broken ankle. That's why he's home right now. Not because of some lady," Pete said, nodding at the two young men. "He's had a long day. He gets tired with that cast on his leg."

After they moved on, Russ and Abby arrived.

"How's the leg doing?" Russ asked at once.

"Fine. Hi, Abby. Good to see you."

"Hi, Rich, Mrs. Dawson, Mr. and Mrs. Randall."

Janie leaned forward. "Make it Pete and Janie, Abby, like I told you. There are too many Randalls around who'll answer to those names."

"I guess you're right. Even Toby and Elizabeth," Abby pointed out. She and Elizabeth both taught at the elementary school. "I'm looking forward to meeting the *future* Mrs. Randall," she said, a big smile on her face as she stared at Rich.

"But that would be you," Rich said.

"No, silly, not me!" Abby exclaimed with a chuckle. "The rumor around town is that you're settling down." She beamed at Rich as if that were a happy thing.

"What are you talking about?" Rich demanded harshly.

Russ leaned closer. "Are we rushing things, bro?" he asked.

"No, you didn't rush things. You just drove off a cliff. Of course I'm not getting married! Don't believe the blasted rumors!"

RESTING IN HER hospital bed, Samantha was still getting over the shock of Rich's kiss. She was replaying the scene in her mind. The look in Rich's eyes as he'd backed away, a stunned expression on his face even as he had pulled her arms from around his neck.

"I gotta go!" Rich had muttered and had quickly disappeared.

Now Samantha closed her eyes, fighting the tears, fighting the throbbing pain. She wasn't sure which hurt the most. The physical pain as her painkiller wore off, or the heartache she felt at Rich's regret over their accidental, magical kiss.

The young nurse who'd given her the water earlier came into the room. One look at Sam's face and she demanded, "What's wrong? Are you in pain? Why didn't you call us?"

Sam opened her eyes. "I just moved wrong. That's all."

"You're probably ready for more medication anyway. I'll check with the doctor."

As the nurse turned to go, Samantha called out to her. "No! No, I'm going to have visitors. I don't want to take anything until it's time to go to sleep." People were actually coming to see her. She'd never had people visit her when she was sick or injured before.

"I'll discuss it with the doctor." Then the nurse disappeared, leaving Samantha alone. With time to think about that kiss...and Rich's reaction. She knew it had been unintentional. And his expression had told her that he hadn't enjoyed it. But she had. That was the scary part. It had to be because of the medication. It couldn't be anything else.

Her door opened and Dr. Jacoby came in.

"I thought doctors didn't work late," Samantha said, trying to mask her pain.

"Only when I have a pretty patient, young lady. How are you doing?"

"Fine."

"Liar." He reached for her left hand and took her pulse. Then he looked at her eyes. "Why didn't you want medication?"

"It puts me to sleep. I haven't eaten dinner and I might have visitors tonight. I've never had visitors, doctor. I—I'm excited about that."

She realized she'd made the doctor feel sorry for her, something she hated, but she had to explain so he wouldn't medicate her.

"The Randalls are a nice family," he said. "Let's make a deal."

"What?"

"I'll give you a little medicine that will ease the throbbing if you promise to lie real still. I want you to even let the nurse feed you. Then as soon as your visitors leave, I'll come give you the rest of your cation.''

"I don't want to make you work late. Can nurse—''

"I live next door. Besides, I want to see if y joyed your visitors. Okay?''

"Thank you, Dr. Jacoby.''

He surprised her by taking her left hand in h gently squeezing it. She smiled back at him as h

"See you in a little while,'' the doctor sai closed the door behind him.

Almost immediately the nurse returned with pill in a small paper cup. She gave it to Samanth got her some water. "Oh! Doc said I should fee Let me go get you a tray. I'll hurry 'cause I'm you're hungry.''

Samantha wasn't sure she could eat. At least no the pill took the edge off her pain.

When the nurse returned Red and Mildred wer her. "I have to feed her, but I'm sure she'd like t with you,'' the nurse told the older couple.

Mildred smiled. "I can feed her so you can break.''

"Are you sure you don't mind? The doctor d want her to move at all.''

"I'll take care of it.'' After the nurse left, M kissed her on the cheek. "I hear you've been brave,'' she said, cupping Samantha's cheek.

Samantha tried to shake her head, but M stopped her. "You're supposed to lie still. Red, y to her while I feed her.''

Mildred started opening up the containers. "Oh, look. You get banana pudding for dessert. That's Red's favorite."

"Red, you can have the pudding. I'm not that hungry," Sam said, not sure she could eat anything.

"Aw, naw. I won't take your pudding. It's the best part," Red protested.

"Aha! She has meat loaf and mashed potatoes and green beans. Here, start off with a bite of meat loaf," Mildred said, offering Samantha a bite on the fork. For the next fifteen minutes, Mildred slowly fed Samantha her dinner and both she and Red chatted with her.

Samantha had never had such loving care. "You're both being so sweet. Red, please eat the banana pudding. I can't eat anymore."

Red's face lit up. "If you're sure..."

Mildred and Samantha shared a smile as Red dug into the banana pudding.

"Hey, who's eating here?" Jake, the oldest of the Randalls, asked as he and his wife B.J. entered the room.

"The little girl said she'd had too much," Red immediately assured Jake.

"Red's helping me out," Sam said with a big smile. The merriment they all shared almost made Samantha forget her pain.

B.J. presented her with a big box of chocolates and Samantha immediately asked Mildred to pass them around so everyone could share.

"Brett and Anna and Chad and Megan will stop by tomorrow. We didn't want to overwhelm you," B.J.

told her with a grin. "It's hard for people to handle all of us at once."

"Oh, please, that's not necessary. You've all been more than generous." She hadn't seen this many Randalls since the meal she shared with all of them that first night she arrived.

Jake leaned over and patted her good hand. "You heard Pete. You're one of our own. How long will you have to stay here? Pete said you wrenched your shoulder as well as getting cut."

"Yes," she said with a sigh. "At first, the doctor said I could go home in the morning, but now he says I'll have to stay a second night."

"One more night won't be too bad," B.J. said.

Samantha smiled, saying nothing.

About that time, Pete, Janie and Lavinia returned, along with a couple. At first Samantha's heart raced, thinking Rich had returned with another woman. But she realized almost at once that it was Russ, not Rich.

"Hi. Um, thank you for coming to visit me," she said, unsure how she should respond.

"Samantha," Russ said, stepping forward and pulling the young woman with him, "I want you to meet Abby, my fiancée. We're getting married in July, on our birthday."

"Oh, a double celebration. How nice!" She smiled and the conversation picked up again. She hoped no one noticed when she kept watching the door. With so many people in the room, no one would realize she was watching for Rich.

Which was foolish. She didn't think he would come

after that fiasco of a goodbye. But she couldn't help herself. After all, he had to catch a ride home. He couldn't drive himself.

Suddenly, Pete said, "Rich had some errands to take care of. He's meeting us here later."

She smiled. It felt stiff, but she was sure no one would notice. "Mildred, please offer them some of the chocolates B.J. and Jake brought."

Pete raised an eyebrow at her. "Chocolates? That was thoughtful," he agreed with a smile.

Samantha felt her cheeks flush. She knew Pete was remembering her remark about staying with the family that first evening when she tried to leave and he and Rich had come after her. When the box came back to her, Samantha deliberately took a chocolate and bit into it. Pleasure filled her.

First the kiss. Now the chocolate. She was in big trouble.

When it came time for everyone to go, Samantha hated to see the end of the visit. She'd enjoyed it a lot. But the pain was coming back and she was going to be ready for another pill when the doctor returned.

She heard his voice in the hall and gave a sigh.

"What's this? A convention of Randalls?" the doctor asked as he entered the room.

"Hey, Doc," Jake said, greeting his old friend. "How's our patient?"

"Pretty tired, I imagine. I'm going to have to run you all out. She's promised to take her pill and go to sleep."

He handed Samantha a large pill and a glass of water.

"I'll send the nurse to help you get settled for bed, young lady."

She nodded dutifully.

All her visitors rose and started filing out, calling good wishes over their shoulders. And Sam couldn't help but wonder why Rich hadn't shown up. How was he going to get home?

Pete was the last one out. He stopped by the bed and proved to her that he'd noticed her concern over Rich's absence. "Don't worry about Rich. We won't leave him stranded."

Samantha nodded and sighed.

RICH NOTICED that his father was frowning when he emerged from the hospital. Leaning against the front fender of his grandmother's car, Rich greeted his grandmother as she got behind the wheel.

Just as Rich opened the passenger side door Pete called out to him. "Rich! Wait a minute, please. Come ride with me. Janie will ride with Lavinia. We'll follow them to the ranch."

Curious, Rich followed his father's suggestion. He couldn't help but wonder what his father was up to.

"You staying at your grandmother's tonight?" Pete asked when they were on the road.

"Yeah, I thought I would. I'm worried she might feel a little afraid."

"You're a good boy, Rich."

"Thanks, Dad."

"Now tell me what happened with you and Samantha when you stayed at the hospital after we left."

Rich sat frozen, staring straight ahead. Finally, he muttered, "Nothing."

"Son, I wouldn't have asked if I didn't know *something* happened."

"It was nothing, Dad."

Pete remained silent.

Finally, Rich said, "I was on my way out and well, all of you had kissed Sam on the cheek. So I leaned over to kiss her, too, and she turned her head."

"You mean you kissed her on the lips?"

"I didn't mean to."

"What did she say?"

"Nothing. I left. How did you know something happened?"

"You weren't exactly in a happy mood when you got to the restaurant. And when we got back to the hospital, I realized Samantha kept looking at the door, like she expected you to come in."

They drove along in silence.

Finally Pete said, "I try not to interfere in your social life, son, but I don't want Samantha upset...or even worse, running away."

"Hey, she's not getting ideas from me!" Rich yelled. "Everyone in Rawhide has assumed I'm marrying her. All I did was bring her to town. I made it clear that all I was offering was a ride."

"Well, make sure everything is clear to Samantha, Rich. She's had a hard life."

"Look, I don't have any problem with Sam hanging around. But I can't have everyone thinking I'm marrying her."

"What would it hurt for a little while? You just got back in town."

"Dad! Look, I'll move over to Grandma's. To watch out for her and Samantha. But I'm making sure Sam understands I'm not interested in—in marrying."

"Don't hurt her feelings."

"No, I won't. But I'll introduce her around. Tell everyone she's like my sister," Rich promised.

Pete noticed some disgust in Rich's voice. "You think the family is too big as it is? That we don't have room for one more?"

"Of course not. Russ and I didn't resent Casey, did we?"

"No. You treated him like a toy. It's a wonder he survived," Pete said with a grin.

"Yeah, we did upset Mom a couple of times, didn't we?" Rich said with a chuckle. "It's just that I'll be lying if I say I think of Sam as one of the family."

"What?" Pete asked, his gaze fixed on his son's face.

"Well, damn it, Dad, I don't plan on marrying Sam, but that doesn't mean I think of her as a sister! She's— I just don't have brotherly feelings for her."

"Yeah." Pete cleared his throat. "Look, son, I want you to know I'm serious about taking care of Samantha. I don't want her back on her own. So...be careful, okay?"

With a big sigh, Rich said, "Sure, Dad. I'll be careful, and I won't hurt her. But I'm not marrying her. I'm not willing to do that."

"I wouldn't ask you to do that, Rich. Unless you fell for her. She's a special lady, you know. Reminds me of your mother. She was a tough customer, too. But she has a big heart. I think Samantha does, too.''

"Dad, you said you weren't matchmaking, remember?''

"I'm not. Are you going into town tomorrow to visit her in the hospital?''

"So the doc is keeping her another night?''

"Appears so.''

"If Grandma wants to go, I'll go with her, but I can't drive.''

"I'll get your mom to come pick you up.''

"Dad—Sam probably doesn't want to see me. I think I embarrassed her.''

"I'll tell your mother to call before she comes.''

Rich gave up.

Chapter Ten

Samantha took her shower the next morning and changed into her white robe and gown. The fact that that much activity exhausted her was frightening. She lay down for a few minutes and had breakfast. Then she got out of bed and walked the halls in the small clinic trying to regain her stamina.

After lunch she walked again. There were several elderly ladies without visitors and Samantha hoped she'd brightened up their day by visiting with them. She had just left one room when the nurse caught up with her.

"You've got visitors, Samantha. Better head back to your room."

Samantha was eager to visit with any of the Randalls, but she figured it was Janie or Lavinia. She was pretty sure it wouldn't be Rich since he'd avoided her last night.

To her surprise, Rich stood by the door and was the first to greet her.

"Afternoon, Sam. We didn't realize you were mobile."

"I'm trying to move around. I'm a little weak from

just lying in bed,'' she told him, restraining from covering herself. The gown and robe combined was opaque, but she was very conscious of not being more formally dressed.

Janie and Lavinia gently hugged her and kissed her cheek. Janie had some beautiful flowers in her hand, and Lavinia had another wrapped package.

"You shouldn't have brought anything. You gave me my lovely gowns yesterday,'' Samantha protested.

Janie put the flowers on her bedside table. "They're just to cheer you up until you come home tomorrow morning.''

It occurred to Sam that she never used the word *home* when she found a temporary place to live. What a glorious word that was: *home*.

"And this reminded me of you,'' Lavinia said with a smile, handing over the present.

Sam opened the box to find a bottle of cologne. She hoped it wasn't one of those heavy, musk-ridden scents. But she should've known better. Lavinia had chosen a clean sunshiny scent that lifted Sam's spirits the moment she smelled it. "Oh, I love this!'' She sprayed a little behind her ears and on her wrists. "Smell!'' she ordered, extending her wrist to Janie.

Janie sniffed and praised her mother's choice. Then she insisted Rich smell. Samantha wanted to draw back her wrist, but she couldn't without being rude. Rich took her hand in his and bent closer to sniff her wrist.

Abruptly, he dropped her hand. "Very nice,'' he said and moved back to lean against the wall, as far away as he could get from Samantha.

Sam chatted with the two ladies, ignoring Rich as he ignored her. It was obvious he hadn't been given a choice about coming. When she mentioned the two ladies she'd been visiting, Lavinia and Janie decided to say hello to them. They ordered Rich to keep her company until they got back.

An awkward silence filled the room.

Finally, Rich pushed away from the wall and said, "We've got to talk."

Samantha tried to square her shoulders, sure he was going to ask her to leave because she'd made him uncomfortable after last night. It was his home, after all. But her right shoulder was still painful. She sank against the pillows. "Of course. I can be on my way day after tomorrow."

"No!" he roared, taking her by surprise.

"You don't want me to leave?"

"*I* don't have anything to do with your decision. But Dad wants you to stay. He's afraid I hurt your feelings last night when I—I didn't intend to kiss you. You turned your head and—it was an accident."

"I know." She kept her voice calm. But the question running over and over again in her head was *I can stay?*

"You do?"

"Of course." She raised her chin a little and issued a brittle laugh, hoping Rich didn't notice. "The look of horror on your face made it obvious."

"I didn't mean— We're causing a lot of gossip."

He sounded grim and Samantha wondered what people were saying.

He didn't wait for her to ask. "They're saying we're

getting married. But you remember I made it clear that wasn't in the cards, don't you?''

''Of course.''

He breathed a sigh of relief. ''Okay. I wanted to make sure you didn't expect me to marry you. Not that there's anything wrong with you. But I'm not the marrying kind.''

''All right.''

''That's all you've got to say?''

''What did you expect me to say? Cry and plead for you to marry me? I never stay where I'm not wanted.''

''Just because I'm not interested in marriage doesn't mean you should go!'' he hurriedly said. ''Dad and Mom want you to stay. Grandma would be devastated if you left. I don't care if you stay. As long as you don't expect me to—uh—''

''Marry me,'' she said.

''Yeah.''

''No problem. If you don't mind, then, I'll stay at least until I'm stronger.''

''Good,'' he said, relief on his face. ''So, I'll be busy, working on the ranch, and you'll be in the house with Grandma. We won't see much of each other and—and the rumors will die out.''

''Right.'' She held on to her emotions, though she admitted to herself it depressed her that he wanted to avoid her. Unconsciously she lifted her wrist to her face and sniffed the perfume again. Maybe she shouldn't have agreed to stay a while. She was noticing a partiality for Rich that was growing. Her eyes widened as she realized it was possible she was coming to care for him.

She closed her eyes, not wanting to let escape any hint of such a fact. The man was already freaked out by the rumors. She'd never lived in a small town, and she had no concept of the gossip that could occur, but Rich seemed fearful of it. As if a rumor of their marrying might *make* him marry her. A ridiculous thought!

While she'd been trying to order her thoughts, Janie and Lavinia came in again.

Janie looked first at Samantha and then Rich. "Did my son prop himself against the wall and not speak while we were gone?"

Rich's face turned red, but Samantha calmly said. "Why, no, he's been telling me about his ideas for his new job. I'm impressed with his knowledge."

"Good," Janie said. "I'd hate to hear he'd been rude."

"Not at all," Sam said, smiling. "We're as comfortable with each other as brother and sister."

Rich glared at her, but she thought it was a nice touch. That would make it clear to everyone that there was no attraction between them. Which was a lie, of course, on her part, but that didn't matter. At least she was going to be able to stay in the first place she'd called home in twenty-four years.

WHEN LAVINIA and Rich drove to town to pick up Samantha the next afternoon, Rich felt relieved about his situation. Samantha hadn't given him any grief about the marriage thing. And now that she was getting out of the hospital, they wouldn't be under the town's eye.

In fact, he could hurry that along by going out with

someone else. He'd always played the field. He could do so again. But he noticed he didn't have any enthusiasm for it.

Okay, so he'd concentrate on his job until he felt differently. Either way, the rumors would stop.

As Lavinia parked the car, she sneezed.

"Bless you, Grandma. Are you coming down with something?"

"I don't know. I felt funny this morning."

"We'd better get you in to see Doc while we're here." His grandmother had caught pneumonia a couple of years ago and his mom always panicked if Lavinia showed any signs of a cold.

"No, no, I'm sure I'm all right. I have to be to take care of Samantha." Lavinia opened her door and got out of the car, only to sneeze again.

Half an hour later, Doc was patting Lavinia on the shoulders. "You let these young people take care of you now, Lavinia. I want you to stay in bed until you're feeling better."

"It's just the sniffles, Doc, and you know it."

"You said the same thing when you had pneumonia. You do as I say or I'm putting *you* in the hospital."

"We'll take care of her, Doc." Rich put his arm around his grandmother.

"Looks like it will be just you. Sam's recovering well, but she won't be up to doing all the work."

"Uh, okay. I'll take care of both of them."

"Good for you. Call me if she feels worse and I'll come see her. We don't want to take any chances."

"Right."

"Are you picking up Samantha now?"

"Yes."

"I've given her some cream to rub on the strained muscles in her shoulder. It will provide some warmth and help her shoulder to heal faster. Make sure someone applies it every night."

Foreboding filled Rich. On her shoulder? Touching her? Rich would do what he had to do, but that task sounded dangerous.

He let his grandmother go ahead of him to Sam's room. He pulled out his cell phone. "Mom, Grandma has a cold and Doc wants her to go to bed and stay there."

"Oh, thank goodness you had Doc check her out."

"Yeah, but I can't—I mean, I can manage, but any help you can give me would be appreciated."

"I'll be at the house when you get there and get Mom settled in bed, and Sam, too. Then I'll make some things for the freezer. Your dad can come for dinner."

"Thanks, Mom."

When he got to the room, his grandmother was fussing, trying to help Samantha. "Grandma, Doc said for you to take it easy."

Samantha, letting Lavinia tie her shoes, jerked back and winced. "What's wrong with Lavinia?"

"Nothing at all, dear. Just ignore the boy."

"Grandma!" Rich turned to Samantha. "She's starting a cold. Since she had pneumonia a couple of years ago, Doc errs on the side of caution."

"Sit down, Lavinia. I'll manage." She got up and took Lavinia's arm and led her to the only chair in the room. In spite of Lavinia's arguments, Samantha had her seated and leaning back.

Rich was grateful. In turn, he took Samantha's good arm and led her to the bed. "I'll tie your shoes. Are you packed?" He knelt in front of her and quickly tied the shoes. Then he looked for her suitcase.

"Yes. The nurse who helped me dress took care of it."

Helped her dress? Surely they wouldn't expect him to— No, they couldn't ask that of him. It would make it tough to ignore Sam if he had to get that close.

"You can't dress yourself?" he asked, trying to make his voice sound calm, but he figured he missed as his grandmother and Sam both stared at him.

Sam spoke first. "Of course I can. But I'm slower. Don't worry. I can take care of myself and Lavinia, too."

"Sure, okay. Ready?"

When they got to the car, the women escorted by Rich, hobbling along on his walking cast, he realized he had another problem. He shouldn't let his grandmother drive. She'd sneezed three more times on their way out to the car. He found a blanket in the trunk and put his grandmother in the back seat, tucking the blanket around her. She was shivering.

"You aren't supposed to drive," Samantha reminded him quietly.

"I know, but if you help me, we can make it." He opened the passenger door for her. "I've got to pick up the prescription Doc gave us. Do you need to get one filled, too?"

"Yes, but—"

"Hand it to me and I'll take care of both of them at once." She did so, and he indicated the front seat. "Sit down. I'll be back in a minute."

When he returned to the car, he explained that, since the car was automatic, he could drive with his left foot. However, he wanted her to sit next to him in case he needed help.

Samantha strapped herself in to the middle seat. "You mean you want me to grab the wheel?"

"No, I want you to press the gas pedal if necessary. You've got two good feet. I've got two good arms. Together we can manage."

She agreed, watching him carefully. Neither of them noticed anyone looking at them until they backed out of the parking place. Someone shouted, then. Rich looked up and saw several of his friends. They were giving him a thumbs-up.

They were that excited that he was driving? Then it hit him. They saw Sam pressed against him and thought their closeness was for romantic reasons, not for driving.

He groaned and shifted against the car door.

"What's wrong?" Sam asked.

"Nothing!" he snapped. Then he apologized. "Sorry, it's my fault. My friends saw us sitting close together and thought—you know."

"So, do you want me to move away?"

"No. It wouldn't be safe."

If he'd been in the car alone, he wouldn't have hesitated to try driving by himself, but with his grandmother sick in the back seat and Sam having already suffered from severe bruising, he didn't want to have a wreck.

The fifteen-minute drive took a little longer because he didn't want to go too fast. But with Sam pressing against him so she could have her foot ready if he needed help, the ride seemed interminable. Her left breast rested against his right arm, soft yet firm, distracting him from the driving. He only hoped she wouldn't notice his response.

He gave thanks that his mother was waiting for them. She hurried out to the car.

"Mom, come on in. I've changed the sheets on your bed. It's all ready for you."

He opened his door to get out, but his mother's next words stopped him. "You two sure are cozy."

Sam spoke up. "Rich isn't supposed to drive with his right foot, so I was helping."

"Oh, you poor dear," Janie exclaimed. "I forgot, since you've been getting around so well."

"That's okay, Mom. We're a house of gimps," Rich joked.

"Well, let's get Grandma in her bed. Rich, can you make her a cup of hot chocolate?"

"Sure." After saying that he realized he had no idea how his mother or his grandmother made hot chocolate. Maybe they had some of those instant packets.

He got Sam's suitcase and followed her into the house. "I'll carry your bag up after I make the chocolate for Grandma."

"Go take the bag up now. I'll make the chocolate," Sam said, surprising him.

"But your arm?"

"I can do it one-handed, except for pouring it into the cup. You'll be back down here by then."

He didn't wait for her to offer twice.

When he came back into the kitchen, he discovered Sam had found a small tray. She put a napkin and a large cup on the tray along with the pills the doctor had prescribed. "Should I add a couple of cookies?" she asked. "Did she eat much lunch?"

Rich scratched the back of his neck. "Come to think of it, she didn't." He had had his mind on picking up Samantha and hadn't paid much attention to his grandmother's appetite. "That's a good idea."

When the chocolate was ready, she had Rich pour it into the large cup. Then she had him pour it into three regular-size mugs. One of them she added to the tray. "For your mother," she said and reached down to slide the tray toward him.

Rich must've thought she was going to try to pick up the tray, because he lunged toward her, reaching out. Samantha tried to back away and lost her footing. Rich grabbed her and pulled her against him.

It was as if the world had stopped spinning suddenly as he held her against him, their breaths mingling as their gazes met.

"Sam, I didn't—" Rich began.

At the same time, Sam said, "I'm sorry—"

They stared at each other and Samantha felt her breath grow shallow, until she couldn't breathe at all as

Rich's mouth covered hers. His strong arms wrapped around her body. Samantha slid her arms around his neck, loving the feel of him pressed against her. The rediscovery of that magic she'd felt before was amazing. She'd told herself she must've imagined it.

He reslanted his lips as they kissed, as if he wanted more. Though Samantha knew there were reasons she shouldn't supply his needs, she couldn't seem to help herself. Or remember why she shouldn't. His touch was too heavenly.

The sound of the creak she always heard when someone was on the fourth step from the top, jerked her back to reality. When Rich pushed her away before she could move, she assumed it did the same for him.

Suddenly she went from the exciting warmth of his body to nothing. They stood there staring at each other, but at least they weren't touching.

Janie breezed into the kitchen. "Did he forget how to make the hot chocolate?" she asked cheerfully. Then her gaze fell onto the tray. "Oh, it's all made. Sorry I misjudged you, son. Were you afraid to carry it up because of your cast?"

"Yes!" Samantha agreed enthusiastically, relieved that Janie came up with a reason for the delay. "Him with his foot and me with my arm, it was hard to decide who would be the biggest risk."

Rich said nothing. He didn't even look at his mother. Fortunately, her mind was preoccupied. "I'll take care of it. Oh, there's a cup for me, too. Thanks, Sam."

Then they were suddenly alone in the kitchen again. A deadly silent kitchen.

Rich ran his fingers through his hair. "I can't keep apologizing!" he finally said, sounding as if he would explode if he didn't say something.

Sam realized she didn't want an apology. What she really wanted was for him to repeat his actions. Her cheeks blazed with fire as she turned away. "It's not necessary."

"Yes, it is! I've told you I won't marry you, but I keep kissing you."

She looked at him questioningly. "You think you have to marry every girl you kiss?"

"No!" he roared.

She immediately shushed him. She didn't want his mother coming down to find out what was wrong. It was bad enough discussing this with Rich, but his mother? "So, we both understand the situation. If one of us—forgets and kisses the other, it's just a passing thing. If no one sees us, then they won't think anything about it. So there's no harm." She wasn't sure she made sense, but she wanted the discussion ended. "I think I'll go lie down for a little while. I'm tired."

Janie reentered the kitchen to hear that remark. "I'm glad you're going to lie down. I came down to tell Rich he had to stop talking so you could rest. But it is good to see how well you two are getting along."

With Janie standing there beaming at them, Samantha didn't dare even glance at Rich. "Right, Janie. I'll go to bed at once." And she bolted from the kitchen.

Chapter Eleven

Since not only Rich's mother but his father also came over to Lavinia's for dinner, everything went smoothly that evening. Rich even had a chance to talk to his dad about some changes he wanted to make to the routine on the ranch.

He and his father did the dishes after dinner. All the kids had been trained in cleanup at home, male and female. His mom had said she wasn't going to raise boys who thought they should be waited on.

While they cleaned the kitchen, Janie first put her mother to bed for the night and then took care of Samantha. Rich gave her the cream before she went upstairs. And breathed a sigh of relief.

Until his father asked him to sit down because they needed to talk.

"Dad, I cleared everything up with Samantha. She's happy to stay and she doesn't expect me to marry her, I swear." He could've said that with a clean conscience this morning, but the afternoon had confused the issue. He wasn't clear on what Sam meant with that jumbled speech before his mom came down. He thought maybe

she was telling him she liked his kisses. But he certai
didn't need to think that!

"Good. Glad to hear it. But that's not what I nee
talk to you about."

"It's not?"

"Nope. Your mom and I didn't go anywhere for
anniversary this year and I felt bad about it. So I bou
tickets for a trip to Hawaii as a surprise."

"Good for you, Dad. That's romantic."

His father grinned. "Yeah. I've learned a little o
the years."

"So when do you— Uh-oh. That's the problem, i
it?" A hard lump settled in his stomach. So much
all his plans to avoid Samantha.

"I'm afraid so, son."

"When?"

"This is Thursday night and we leave Satur
morning." Pete stared at his son. "What I need to kr
is, can you manage with the two ladies upstairs by y
self?"

Rich knew what his father wanted to hear. And
was going to give him that answer, no matter what.
parents were the best. "Sure, I can. We'll be fine."

"Are you sure, son?"

"Yeah, I'm sure."

"I'll get Anna to come by and check on you w
she can. And Russ and Abby will spend the week
with you. I'm sure Mildred will send over some meal

"That's nice. Then I'm sure we can make it."

"Your mother will probably call here every day
be sure they're all right. Any trouble and you can

ways call the ranch and whoever's available will be right over.''

Rich couldn't help but smile. What his dad said was true. But he couldn't see calling any of the uncles to come rub Sam's shoulder. "I know. We'll be fine. I'm pretty sure Grandma just has a cold. But we won't take any chances, I promise."

"What do you promise?" Janie asked as she entered the kitchen.

"To take care of Grandma and Sam."

"Of course you will," she said with a smile, "but I'll be here."

"No, you won't, sweetheart," Pete said.

"What are you talking about, Pete?"

"I'm talking about tickets I already bought for us to fly to Hawaii Saturday morning."

Janie gasped. "But why?"

"Because I haven't had you to myself in a while. Plus, it's a belated anniversary present."

"But Mom—"

"Will be taken care of," Rich quickly said, thinking his mother looked like a newlywed as she stared at her husband. The love they shared had always been strong. The boys had never doubted it when they were growing up.

"What if she gets worse? I'll admit she just seems to have a cold, but—"

"First we'll call Doc to come see her. Then we'll call you and I bet Dad will get you back here as soon as possible. It's not like you're abandoning her. She's got me and Sam and the rest of the family," Rich assured her.

"Oh, Pete, you know I want to go," Janie said with tears in her eyes.

"I know, honey, but if it upsets you too much, we won't go," Pete hurriedly said.

"Why don't you bring Anna over tomorrow to look at Grandma and see what she thinks?" Rich suggested.

"Good idea, Rich," Pete said and turned to his wife. "And on the way home I'll tell you about the other arrangements I've made."

Rich escorted his parents to the door and stood there watching them drive off. Then he banged his head against the wood frame of the door. "Good Lord, what have I done?" he asked himself.

THE NEXT MORNING when Samantha first opened her eyes, she smelled coffee and bacon. She almost turned over to sleep a little longer until they delivered breakfast to her room.

Then she remembered she wasn't in the hospital any longer. And Rich had to be the one doing the cooking. She shoved back the cover and got out of bed. She dressed slowly but she noticed the pain wasn't quite as bad today.

Before she came to the hospital yesterday, Lavinia had found some button-up shirts in her closet that she had put in Samantha's room, knowing they'd be easier for her to wear as long as her shoulder was painful.

She opened Lavinia's door before she went downstairs, but the older woman was still asleep. When Sam reached the kitchen, she discovered Rich sitting at the table eating. "Is there any extra?" she asked apologetically.

He stood. "Sure. I made enough for all of us. I was trying to decide if I should wake you."

He fixed a plate for Samantha and brought it to the table. "You want milk, juice or coffee?"

Samantha chose milk. He set a glass down beside her plate and then resumed his own place. After several minutes of eating, Samantha said, "You're a good cook, Rich."

"Thanks. Mom raised us to take care of ourselves. I'm just not sure my skills would impress either you or Grandma."

"I'm sure you'd manage, but you won't have to. I'm doing better and Red and Mildred have promised to send over some food."

"I'm glad you feel that way, 'cause Dad is taking Mom to Hawaii on Saturday."

Sam's head snapped up. "What?" They were both being unfailingly polite, but Rich was keeping his distance. She'd figured they could manage what little time they spent together, but news that they would be alone scrambled her insides.

"It's a belated anniversary present. He's already bought the tickets. I told Mom we'll be okay."

"Of course we will. How wonderful! Your father is a great man," Samantha replied. She'd always thought Hawaii was the ultimate romantic place, one she'd never see.

"Nice of you to say that. It's going to mean more work for you when you're not in the best shape."

"I'll manage." She wasn't concerned about any extra work. Lavinia had given her a home. She'd do what needed to be done. And keep away from Rich.

Rich frowned. "Hey! Where's the sling the doc said you should wear?"

"It's hard to get on by myself. Besides, I don't really need it."

"You need it. You could pull your stitches loose. Where is it?"

"It's in my room, but I can—" She stopped because he was no longer there. She could hear his steps on the stairs.

She stood and carried the dishes to the sink, using only her left hand. Then she got out a tray and fixed a plate for Lavinia. She had it ready to go when Rich returned to the kitchen.

"This tray is ready, if you can carry it up. Then we'll let you get to your real job." She smiled, appreciating his work this morning.

"First your sling. Come here."

She couldn't argue, but it made her anxious to get that close to him. Keeping her head down, she stood in front of him. He lifted the sling over her head, sliding the straps onto her shoulders before he gently placed her bruised and cut arm into the sling.

Samantha raised her head to thank him, to find her lips only inches from his. She pulled back even as he lowered his lips to hers. Shocked, she started to protest when the back door opened.

Janie stared at the two of them. "Everything okay?"

"Fine," Samantha hurriedly said. "Rich was helping me get my sling on."

"I'm glad to see he's doing his best for you," Janie said, grinning.

"He is. He got up early and prepared breakfast for all of us. I just fixed Lavinia's tray."

"Is she awake?" Janie asked.

"No, but I thought she shouldn't miss meals."

"You're right. I'll take the tray up. Rich, you can do your own job today. After I'm gone you may have to cut back, but today you get to be a cowboy, not a nursemaid."

Janie picked up the tray and hurried up the stairs.

Sam took several steps away from him. "Will you be in for lunch? Your mother will want to know."

"Yeah, probably."

"Don't overdo it, today."

"I don't need a second mother," he returned, glaring at her.

"And you don't need a wife. I think we all get the picture, so don't gripe at me."

His cheeks flushed a bright red and he turned and strode out of the house.

Samantha sat down at the table and reached for the coffeepot. She needed another cup of coffee.

RICH KEPT HIS thoughts at bay until he'd saddled his favorite gelding and swung into the saddle. He could just get the cast into the stirrup, so he was careful not to take risks. He didn't want any more injuries.

Once the horse was in motion, heading toward the north pasture, Rich let his mind go back to the kiss that didn't happen. What was wrong with him?

He'd tried to establish a nonromantic relationship with Samantha. But every time he was alone with her, he couldn't seem to keep his hands off her. This morning he'd been determined to show that he could be in the room with her and not—not attack her. Then he'd almost given in to temptation. Those "accidental kisses" had him hungering for more. But it didn't have him wanting anything permanent.

He was an idiot! If he gave in to temptation, he would be marching down the aisle whether he wanted to or not. His father would see to it. So, he'd keep his distance. That was all it would take. And maybe he felt like dating some town girl just for fun, after all.

That's what he'd do. And he wouldn't think about Samantha. He picked up speed, hoping to outrun his thoughts.

When he headed for the house at the end of the day, without coming in for lunch, he was dead tired. But they'd come across a cow having delivery difficulties with an early calf. But they'd saved them both. So he'd had a successful day, but he was late.

At least he didn't have to worry about getting in early. His mom was there to tend to Grandma and Sam. He'd grab something to eat and a hot shower and then hit his bed. He suspected he'd be asleep before he could pull up the cover.

One of his men offered to ride with him to the house so he could take Rich's horse back to the barn and rub him down. Rich had been taught to tend to his own animals, but he thought even his dad would forgive him tonight.

"Thanks, Doyle. I owe you one," he said as he slid from the saddle.

"No problem, boss. You overdid it today. But you sure were a help. Couldn't have managed everything without you." The cowboy nodded in the fading light and headed for Lavinia's barn, leading Rich's horse.

Rich limped across the porch into the house.

When he reached the kitchen, he discovered Samantha had set the table for two. As he came in, she pulled a small casserole dish from the oven awkwardly, barely using her right hand. The casserole tilted dangerously and he sprang forward.

"Don't! It's hot," Sam muttered, shifting the dish away from him and sliding it onto the table.

"I thought you were going to drop it," he exclaimed.

She gave him a brief smile before opening the fridge and bringing out a tossed salad.

Rich stood there, watching her, feeling useless and awkward.

"Sit down."

"I need to wash up." He spun around and hurried to the workroom nearby. By the time he got back to the kitchen, hot rolls were on the table, along with glasses of iced tea.

Sam gestured for him to sit down and joined him at the table. "Don't forget to leave room for Red's famous chocolate cake. He sent one over today."

As he was filling his plate, Rich asked, "Where's Mom? Is she eating with Grandma?"

The only answer he got was a shake of Sam's head. She concentrated on her dinner.

"Sam? Where's Mom?"

"She went home early. I told her we could manage and she hadn't packed yet."

"She went home early?" he asked, his appetite suddenly going away. What about Sam's shoulder cream? Was his nightmare coming true? Would she expect him to rub her shoulder, her bare skin?

"Don't worry. Everything's taken care of. Your aunt Anna came by today and said Lavinia was doing very well. She's coming back tomorrow to check on her again. Your family is so incredibly nice."

"Yeah," Rich agreed, still thinking about the rest of the evening. So much for going straight to bed.

When he'd finished his dinner, Samantha asked, "Do you want your cake now? Or shall I bring it in while you're watching TV? Janie said one of your favorite shows comes on tonight."

He couldn't remember a television show that he watched frequently. Certainly not one that would take his mind off Samantha. "Uh, let's do the dishes and then have cake."

"You don't have to do the dishes, Rich. You worked all day, without lunch."

"Uh, I apologize for not making it in. But we had an early calf that demanded our attention." He didn't see any anger or pouting on her face for his failure to appear.

"Is it all right?" she asked, concern on her beautiful face. It amazed him how pretty she could look with no makeup, her hair pulled back in a ponytail.

He cleared his throat. "Uh, yeah, it's fine."

"Good," she said with a smile and stood to clear the table.

He picked up his own dishes and followed her to the sink. He waited until she'd awkwardly rinsed her own and then stepped forward to rinse his.

"I'll do that," Sam protested.

"Look, Sam, I know you'd do it. I know you're a hard worker. You don't have to prove anything to me. So relax. We'll work together."

She stood still for a minute. Then she smiled at him, a warm smile that lit up her face. "Thank you, Rich."

When he'd finished rinsing the other dishes, he said, "Sit down. I'll cut the cake."

While they ate the sinfully rich chocolate cake, Samantha asked questions about his day. He found himself describing the baby calf and its difficult introduction to life. Her laughter and interest eased the tiredness from his body.

They cleaned up the last dishes, leaving the kitchen as clean as Lavinia liked it.

Rich took a last look. "Nice job, partner."

"Same to you," she said with a smile. "I'm going to give Lavinia her pill and settle her in for the night."

"I'll come with you and tell her good-night."

"I'm sure she'll like that."

When Rich opened the door to his grandmother's

room, she was already dozing, propped against two pillows, the television playing.

"Oh, dear. I hate to wake her but she has to have her pill," Sam said.

"It's okay. She'll go right back to sleep. Grandma?" Lavinia's lashes fluttered. "Is that you, Rich?"

"Yes, ma'am, it is. Sorry I got in so late."

"I 'spect you were busy. Your grandpa used to run late some nights."

"I came to give you a good-night kiss." He bent down and put his lips on her weathered skin and brushed back her hair from her face. "Are you behaving yourself so you'll get well?"

"Yep. Janie and Sam don't give me a choice." But she wasn't complaining. She sent a loving look at Samantha.

"Sam's going to help you to bed, and I'll get in early tomorrow, okay?"

"'Kay." She smiled sweetly.

Rich walked to the door. "I'm going to grab a shower if that's okay."

"Of course."

He started to say, "Come get me if you need me," but that thought was a dangerous one. "I'll hurry," he said instead and scooted out of the room.

After his shower, which helped revive him slightly, he put on clean jeans, along with a clean T-shirt, and carried his dirty clothes to the laundry room.

He found Sam in the kitchen. He stood at the door and watched her take a pill. Which reminded him of the shoulder cream. "Are you going to be able to rub that cream into your shoulder?"

He could tell he'd startled her. "Oh— Yes, of course, I'll manage."

She was lying and they both knew it. "Are you taking a shower?"

She nodded, her eyes wide. Beautiful green eyes.

"When you're out of the shower, wrap a big towel around you and call me. I'll come rub it in."

"I don't think that's a good idea."

He didn't ask why. He knew the reasons even better than she. "I promised Mom I'd take care of you as well as Grandma. Everything will be fine. It won't take but a minute."

He'd make sure of that.

When he heard her softly call, as if she were hoping he wouldn't hear her, he knocked on her bedroom door. He'd lectured himself the entire time he waited and he was prepared to touch her.

The first sight of her told him he was mistaken. Her slender shoulders, one black and blue, the other a creamy pink, were exposed over the bath towel she'd wrapped around herself. Her long dark hair was loose and forming an enticing curtain about her shoulders.

"Shall—shall I sit on the bed?" she asked, avoiding his gaze.

"No! No, it'll be easier if you sit on the vanity bench." Something the two of them couldn't fit on at the same time.

She reached out to the vanity and handed him the tube. "Here's the cream."

"Okay." He read the directions carefully, trying to delay touching her. Finally, he had no excuse to postpone the massage. He squirted the proper amount of cream into his hand and then gently touched her skin. In spite of the bruising, her skin was soft, warm, wonderful.

His hands slid over her shoulder, down her back and up again. He remained standing, which allowed him to stare down at the shadowy cleft where she'd tucked in the towel. His breathing sped up and he looked away, hoping she wouldn't notice. He hurriedly covered the bruised area two more times, but he couldn't hold his breath any longer.

"I hope that will do. I'm not very good with my hands," he said, then turned bright red. The innuendo hadn't been intended. He stepped back, his hands in the traditional surrender position. "Uh, is there anything else you need done before I go?"

"No, thank you," she said.

He was pleased to notice that she sounded a little out of breath, too. He didn't want to be the only one to suffer.

"I'm going right to bed as soon as you leave," she said pointedly, staring at the door.

"Oh, oh yeah. I'm going to bed, too."

"You don't have to cook for us in the morning. I'll wait until Lavinia awakens and cook then. But be sure to eat breakfast yourself."

"Yeah, I will," he promised, backing to the door, taking one more look at her. Then he bumped into the door and almost lost his footing.

"Are you all right, Rich?" Samantha asked. She jumped up and then grabbed her towel as it started a fast descent.

They stood there frozen in time, she protecting her modesty and he leaning against the door, praying the towel would fall away.

Then she said, "Good night."

With that pointed phrase, he turned the doorknob and stepped into the hall, closing the door behind him. Then he bent to his knees, gulping air, wondering if he should shower again, this time with cold water.

Chapter Twelve

The next two weeks passed by more quickly tha
could've imagined. He and Samantha worked ou
tine that got the job done. She seemed to antici
needs and never complained if he didn't make i
dinner on time.

Rich tried to take the pressure off her, lending
every chance he could. The only problem they h
actual physical contact. He hadn't had to rub her
der again. Sam got a female visitor to apply the
before he returned in the evenings. At least she s
did.

They both realized the one time had been a clo
He still had dreams about the towel falling to th
In his dreams, they both ended up on the bed.

Unfortunately, at that point, he always woke

By the end of the two weeks, she was almo
to normal. In addition, Lavinia, though still ta
daily nap, showed no signs of pneumonia. She w
pier than Rich had seen her in a long time. It
Sam spent part of her morning knitting under La
supervision. And she'd stopped Red and Mildre

sending over food, except for Red's chocolate cake. Instead, Sam cooked some of Lavinia's favorite recipes.

Tomorrow his mom and dad would be home, and he would welcome them with no disasters at hand. He'd gotten used to riding with a cast. Each morning he'd put a plastic bag over his cast and taped it so it stayed dry.

"Boss?" one of his cowboys called, jerking him back to reality.

"Yeah?"

The man didn't bother speaking. He nodded to the west. Black clouds topped the peaks in the distance, and appeared to be moving toward them quickly.

"Damn!" Rich muttered to himself. He'd forgotten to listen to the weather report this morning. He'd had his mind on Samantha. "Looks like a bad one," he called to the cowboy. "Thanks."

He took a minute to think about what he needed to do. He was two men short today. One had asked for the day off for personal reasons, and another had turned up sick. He had two big herds he needed to move closer to the house. One was in a southern pasture with a creek that tended to flood. The other was in a higher up pasture, more susceptible to lightning.

He rode over to Tom Jenkins, one of the ranch hands. "I'm going to go call next door and see if they've got any spare men. You take Larry with you and head for the south pasture. Tell Doyle and Bart to move the herd into the open pasture, then head for the north pasture."

"Will do."

He'd been impressed with the hands his grandmother

employed. They took orders well and did their jo[
ficiently. He hurried his horse toward the bar[
hadn't even brought the cell phone with him t
things had gone so well.

Big mistake. He knew better. It was going tc
him an hour to go to the house and get back.

SAM HAD JUST put in a load of laundry and starte
washer when lightning flashed outside the wi[
Startled, she looked out. She'd been busy this mo[
making sure the house was spotless.

"Lavinia?" she called as she walked back to th[
where Lavinia was watching one of the morning s[
"There's a big storm in the west. Lots of lightni[

Lavinia hurried her way. "How big?"

"It looks monstrous. But I'm not used to we
here."

"Some of our spring storms can be bad. Did
have everyone saddled up today?"

Sam thought back to an early-morning call. "[
know he let one man off work today because his[
went to the hospital to have their baby. And this [
ing, one of the men woke up sick."

"Oh, dear. He'll need help."

She picked up the phone and called the R[
ranch. "Red? You've seen the storm? You go[
spare men? Okay. Thanks anyway. No, I'm sure
will manage."

"They can't help out?" Sam asked, even th[
she'd already figured the answer.

"They're shorthanded, too, and everyone's already out."

Sam hesitated, but then she said, "I can ride. If you think you'll be okay here, I can ride out."

Lavinia frowned. "I'd be fine but that's too dangerous for you."

"I'll be okay. Do you have an extra rain slicker and maybe a hat?"

"Of course. What size boot do you wear?"

"Size eight." Sam figured she'd make do with her tennis shoes, but Lavinia beamed at her.

"Me, too, I'll get my boots."

In no time, Sam was completely covered, had eaten a sandwich since it was almost lunchtime, and, after hugging Lavinia, hurried to the barn to saddle up.

She was almost ready to go when she heard the sound of a horse running. She hurried to the door of the barn and pushed it open. Rich rode in out of the rain.

"Are you all right?" she asked, frowning with worry.

"Yeah, but I need more riders if I can find them at Dad's." He swung down from the horse, dripping water everywhere, heading for the phone in the tack room.

"They don't have any," Sam said.

"How do you know?" he demanded, coming to an abrupt halt.

"Lavinia already called. But I'm ready to go."

"Go where?" he asked, dumbfounded.

"To help. Lavinia even lent me her boots."

"You can't go out there. It's too dangerous."

"I certainly can. I know how to ride. And you've

been helping me the past two weeks. It's my turn to return the favor.''

"What about Grandma? She can't be left alone."

"She's well. She insisted I go."

"Sam—" he began, still determined she wouldn't be going.

Before he could even get started, she swung into the saddle and hollered, "Last one out shuts the door." Then she rode out into the storm.

"Damn it!" Rich yelled after her, but he mounted his horse and pulled the barn door closed after he got out into the storm.

He caught up with Sam, who didn't know which direction to go, and he caught the reins and pulled her to a stop.

"Okay, but you stick close to me and do exactly as I say!" He had to yell to be heard over the sounds of the rumbling thunder, but he would've yelled anyway.

She flashed him a smile and reached into her slicker coat and pulled out an apple, tossing it to him. "A snack!"

He muttered, "Thanks," and led the way toward the north pasture.

Several hours later, he led the way back to the barn. When they'd reached the north pasture, he'd sent Bart to help the other two men to the south. He wasn't sending Samantha off by herself. The riding in the north pasture had been tricky because of the rocks and bushes and uneven ground, but Sam had managed fine.

In fact, Doyle hadn't even realized Sam was a woman. When they had secured the herd and called it quits, he'd complimented her. "Hey, cowboy, you really know how to ride."

"Thanks," she'd said and Doyle almost fell out of the saddle.

When they reached the barn, Rich said, "Thanks for the hard work, Doyle. You did a good job today."

He discovered the man was staring at Sam. He cleared his throat. "Are the others in?"

"I reckon," Doyle said. "That's Bart's horse." He pointed out one of the stabled horses. Then he looked at Samantha again. "Who are you?" he asked.

"Samantha Jeffers, Mrs. Dawson's companion."

Rich stared at the cowboy. But Doyle only said she rode as good as a man, high praise from a cowboy. Then he offered to rub down her horse if she wanted to go to the house.

Sam hesitated. "Do you mind? I had to leave Lavinia alone and I'd like to check on her."

"Go on, Sam. We'll be okay," Rich ordered.

She slipped out of the barn, back into the rain, and disappeared from view.

Doyle was much more vocal once Sam was gone. And for a guy who was supposed to think of her as a member of the family, Doyle's appreciation of Sam's talents rubbed Rich the wrong way.

LAVINIA WAS NOT only fine, she'd also prepared a big pot of stew. It was early April, but the rain had been cold and the wind brutal. The moment Sam smelled the aroma, she felt a lot better.

"Lavinia?" she called as she hung the slicker and hat in the workroom.

Lavinia appeared in the doorway to the kitchen. "Is everything all right? Where's Rich?"

"He's in the barn. One of the men offered to rub down my mare so I could come check on you. Did you manage all right?"

"Yep. Felt good, like I was contributing to our success. After my husband died, I didn't have anything to do with the operation. Pete and Janie made decisions and I didn't even have anyone to cook for."

"My nose tells me that's a shame. Something smells really good."

"I'll put the rolls in and we'll be ready to eat in five minutes."

"You haven't eaten yet?"

"Don't worry. I had a piece of cake about four."

Lavinia hurried back to the kitchen while Sam washed her hands and dried her hair with a towel. About the time she finished, Rich came in. She hung up his slicker and hat as he washed up.

"It got pretty cold today," she said. "I wasn't expecting that."

"We've even had some snow in late April. It's no surprise."

"Lavinia's got a hot meal ready. Be sure to praise her. It made her feel good to play a role again," Sam said quietly.

Rich frowned and stared at her. "What do you mean?"

"It makes a person feel good to be needed."

"Speaking of being needed, you were. I didn't expect you to have to ride herd, but you did a good job."

"Thanks," she said with a smile and turned to head for the kitchen.

He followed her. After greeting his grandmother, he sat down at the table. "Grandma, supper smells wonderful. It's good to get warm again."

"I figured you'd be cold. How long do you think this storm will last?"

Rich shrugged. "I don't know. Have you listened to a weather report?"

"No. I got busy making dessert. Hot peach cobbler with ice cream. Your favorite, Rich."

"I'm ready for it. We'll watch the late news to see what they say…after we enjoy our dessert."

After the television weatherman predicted the storms would move out early in the morning, Lavinia and Samantha said good-night and climbed the stairs together. Rich stood at the bottom of the stairs, watching them go.

He felt more content tonight than he ever remembered. He'd done good work today. He'd had a satisfying meal. With good company. Only one thing could make it better.

If he was the one climbing the stairs with Samantha. Sharing her bed. Waking up beside her in the morning.

He knew he was in trouble. He couldn't seduce Samantha. Not when she was under his father's protection. He'd be married in no time. His father would march him down the aisle, whether he wanted to marry or not. Then he'd be locked in, all his choices gone. He couldn't— He stared up at the empty stairs, suddenly realizing he didn't want anything in his life different.

He didn't yearn for the rodeo. He didn't long for the women who offered themselves to the latest winner. He didn't want to pack up every week and move on down the road.

Home. He was where he wanted to be. And somehow he didn't mind Samantha being in the picture. They'd worked well together. He trusted her, admired her work ethic. Admired her body.

He shook himself. What was wrong with him? He was supposed to think of her as his sister. Sister, hell! He thought of her as his dream lover. And his dad was coming home tomorrow.

He was in big trouble.

SAMANTHA LOVED being part of the welcoming party to greet Janie and Pete. She'd even talked Lavinia into joining her and Rich in driving over to the Randalls' ranch to see them as soon as they arrived. She knew Janie wouldn't relax until she'd checked on her mother, even though they'd called numerous times.

Sam found the number of boisterous, vibrant people to be a little overwhelming. She leaned against the wall of the kitchen, watching the others mill about, exchanging conversation. She couldn't even identify half the people there.

Rich had mentioned some of his cousins were in from university. And his father's cousin and his wife and children. Maybe there were some neighbors there, too. How amazing to be surrounded by such a large crowd.

After a few minutes, she moved a few feet closer to another woman she'd seen earlier. She didn't appear to be one of the boisterous Randalls, with their dark or sometimes auburn hair, and big smiles and even bigger personalities. This lady was slender, with pale-blond hair and blue eyes. Samantha thought she'd found someone else who was an outsider.

After greeting the woman, Sam asked. "Are you as overwhelmed as I am?"

The young lady looked at her, a frown on her face. "Overwhelmed? No, I'm used to them all."

"Oh, I'm sorry. I thought you were new to the crowd, too."

With a smile, the woman shook her head. "No. I was born here. I'm a Randall, too."

Sam couldn't hide her surprise. "You're a Randall?"

"I know. It's hard to believe, isn't it? My sister's over there talking to Casey. People never believe we're even kin. I'm Victoria. Anna and Brett are my parents. Mom always says I look like her mother."

Samantha looked from Victoria to the young lady she pointed out as her sister, Jessica. The younger lady had auburn hair and dark-brown eyes. She drew attention easily. "Wow. You really are different from each other, aren't you?"

"Oh, yes. Do you have brothers and sisters?"

"No. I'm Samantha Jeffers. I'm staying with Lavinia to help out."

Victoria smiled. "Oh, you're Rich's girlfriend."

Sam felt her cheeks burn. "No! No, he gave me a ride, but that's all."

A tall handsome Randall crossed the room and slid his arm around Victoria's waist. "You doing okay, Tori?"

"Fine, Jim. Have you met Samantha?"

"Rich's girlfriend? No, I haven't. Glad to meet you, Samantha. Heard you're a good rider."

Samantha had no idea who he was. "How did you hear that?" she asked, not bothering to say anything about Rich and her.

"Rich was bragging on you. I'm Jim, by the way. Elizabeth's brother, Chad and Megan's second child. It gets a little confusing, doesn't it? I suggested we put a chart on the wall so we could all remember who we are, but Uncle Jake wouldn't hear of it."

Samantha laughed along with Jim and Victoria, but she thought that might not be a bad idea. "There are a lot of you."

"Well, almost all of us are here. Drew and Josh didn't come home. They're freshmen. Josh has a test on Monday and he decided to stay and study for it. And Drew, well, there's this girl..." he trailed off and grinned at Tori.

"There always is," she murmured. "But you forgot John and Melissa." She smiled at Sam. "They're our second cousins. Uncle Griff and Aunt Camille are the couple talking to Uncle Chad and Aunt Megan in the corner. It gets a little complicated, but he's our dads' cousin and she is Aunt Megan's stepsister."

"I see...I think."

Tori smiled. "You'll get used to them all. And when I'm here, you can always ask me who's who."

"Thanks, but unless you come home often, I'll probably be gone before I see you again," Sam said.

Tori and Jim exchanged a look of surprise. Then Tori said, "Well, I hope that's not true. It's nice to have someone else around who isn't a carbon copy of the rest of them to keep me company. Don't you like…living with Lavinia?"

"Very much so. She's wonderful. I've never had a grandmother and it's—incredible. But she doesn't really need me, you know. Pete just manufactured that story to give me a break. She's teaching me to knit."

"I should take lessons, too. Then I could do something useful while I'm studying," Tori said with a grin.

"Isn't studying enough to be productive?" Sam asked, a touch of envy she couldn't hide. She'd spent a lot of time in libraries, reading, trying to educate herself, but she'd never had the opportunity to go to college.

"Oh, you know how it is. You have to do a lot of memory work, so I could practice while I knit," Tori said with a smile.

"No, I don't know. I've never been to college," Sam said. She figured all these educated people would turn up their noses at her.

"Don't worry. You're not missing all that much," Tori said. Her words comforted Sam.

"How you doing?" Rich asked, suddenly appearing at Sam's elbow.

Startled, she turned to stare at him, wondering if she'd done something wrong. "F-Fine."

Jim laughed. "Come on, Rich, you know I'm going to hit on your girlfriend. Relax."

That remark effectively halted the conversation both she and Rich turned red. Sam didn't know wh say.

Tori slapped Jim's arm and told both of the m go away. She and Sam were getting to know each Fortunately, they followed her advice and Rich come near Sam the rest of the night.

When it got late and Lavinia was looking tire mantha slipped over to Janie's side and told her sh taking Lavinia home now.

"Is Rich going with you?" Janie asked.

"I haven't asked him. He seems to be enjoyin cousins. He may want to stay later."

Janie waved Rich over and asked him if he was with Sam and Lavinia.

Rich turned to stare at Sam. "I came with th reckon I'll go home with them. Why wouldn't I?"

Sam said nothing. She got the sudden feeling Rich was spoiling for a fight. Had the two wee being on his good behavior been too much?

"Good. I don't like them being out at night wi a man along," Janie said with a grin. "Okay, let get Mom to the car."

Lavinia sitting nearby, stood. "I can get myse the car. There's nothing wrong with me except wa to go to sleep in my own bed."

Pete came over and kissed Lavinia's cheek, pre to walk his mother-in-law out to the car. After he h Lavinia up into Rich's truck, he turned to Samanth heard about yesterday. Rich said you're a great rider. I should've known.''

''It was fun,'' she assured him, a big smile on her face.

''And Rich didn't give you any trouble while we were gone?''

''Hey!'' Rich protested, having overheard his father.

''Not at all. He was very helpful.''

''Glad to hear it.''

''Mom seems very happy,'' Janie added, hugging Samantha. ''Thank you for taking care of her.''

''She's easy to take care of.''

Pete chuckled. ''I've been around her when she was sick before. I know better than that.''

''She was. My knitting has really improved and she taught me some new recipes, too,'' Samantha assured them, still smiling as the three of them walked around the truck to the driver's side.

Rich, already seated on the passenger side by Lavinia, leaned past her and called, ''Are you coming or not?''

''My passengers are impatient, so I'll say good-night. Welcome home,'' she said as she hopped up in the truck.

''I'll see you tomorrow,'' Janie called out.

She and Pete stood arm in arm, watching them as they drove away.

''What do you think?'' Pete asked.

''About Mom? She's happier than I've seen her in a while,'' Janie said, her gaze still on the brake lights of the truck.

"You're right, but that's not what I meant."

Janie looked up at her husband. "You mean Rich and Samantha?"

"Yeah. Is there any interest there?"

"Oh, there's interest. Didn't you see him watching her all evening?"

"But she didn't look at him," Pete pointed out, frowning.

"Even more significant. She was aware of him every minute, but made sure no one else would notice."

"But you noticed," Pete said with a grin.

"Yes. Because I'm his mother. Of course I noticed." She stood there, tapping her lips with her forefinger. "And tomorrow, I intend to find out just how far their relationship has progressed."

"You think he's considering marriage?"

"I don't know. Maybe."

"I'll have a talk with him."

Jake came out on the back porch. "Didn't you two get enough of being alone? Come on back in."

"We're coming, Jake," Janie said. "We were just discussing things."

"You mean, how Rich is crazy about Samantha?"

Pete and Janie walked back toward him. "Why do you think that?" Pete asked.

"The boy didn't leave the ranch once while you were gone. Even after Lavinia was on the mend. Some of the kids called him about going into town last Saturday night, but he refused. Said he had to take care of Sam and Lavinia. So Jim, who was home for the weekend then, too, asked if Samantha wanted to go to town. Rich about bit his head off.''

''We figured you and B.J. or Brett and Anna might've gone over to visit a few times,'' Janie said.

''We thought they might enjoy being alone. Anna checked during the day. Red and Mildred kept them supplied with food. Megan took by some fresh flowers. B.J. checked on a mare due to foal. We took care of them. But we didn't crowd them.''

''Well, we appreciate the effort, Jake,'' Pete said, grinning.

''By the way, brother,'' Jake added, ''we'll take care of the Sunday chores. Consider yourself still on vacation until Monday morning.''

''Thanks. This time-change stuff is hard.''

Jake laughed. ''Yeah, that's the way it is for you jet-setters!'' With a chuckle, he went back inside.

''He's matchmaking, isn't he?'' Janie asked.

''You know he is. But so are you.''

''I am not! That is, I'd be happy if Rich married Sam, but I'm not forcing him into anything.''

''Neither is Jake.''

''Ha! I know how Jake Randall works, Pete. And so do you. You make sure he doesn't play any tricks.''

''Jake's got a good heart,'' Pete said, wrapping his arms about his wife, pulling her back to lean on his chest. They stood there in contentment.

''You know,'' Pete finally said softly, ''Hawaii is beautiful, and I loved every minute we had together, but I sure am glad to be home. Those mountains look pretty good tonight.''

Janie sighed. "You're right. Hawaii is a good place for a visit, but nothing is better than home…and family. We're spoiled."

"Nope. We're blessed. And I hope our children are, too."

"They will be. Abby looked so happy tonight. Russ, too. He held her hand the entire evening. I think Rich wanted to stake a claim, too, but he and Sam haven't progressed that far."

"What about Casey?"

"Oh, Pete, he's just a baby!" Janie protested. "He's got plenty of time yet."

"You're going to have to stop calling him a baby. He hates it."

"Too bad. He has to be my baby until I've got grand-kids."

"That may not be too long from now. Come on, let's go to bed. You heard Jake. I'm still on vacation for another twenty-four hours."

AFTER LAVINIA had gone to bed, Sam came back down the stairs. She wanted to make sure Rich didn't think she'd said anything to make Jim think she was Rich's girlfriend, as he'd put it.

She found Rich sitting in the kitchen, drinking a cup of coffee. "Rich, are you busy?"

He looked up in surprise. "No. Just relaxing a bit. Is Grandma okay?"

"Yes, she's already asleep. I wanted to tell you I didn't say anything to make people think we were— you know, together."

Rich shook his head. "I know. You're talking about Jim, aren't you?"

She nodded. "And Tori. She said something about us being a couple and I told her no. I'm beginning to think matrimony is all your family thinks about!"

"You could be right. But as long as you and I understand—"

"You don't have to tell me again," she interjected, impatience in her voice. "I know you're not interested in marriage. I think I have it etched in my brain now, thank you."

He studied his coffee cup. "When I said that—I mean, I'm not ready yet. That's what I mean. I intend to marry one day. To have a family. But Dad didn't marry until after he was thirty. I'm only twenty-six."

"Right. Well, I just wanted you to know I didn't cause them to think that way." She turned to leave.

"Why don't you have a cup of coffee and join me?"

She was stunned by his invitation. During the past two weeks they'd worked together well. But they'd both avoided any private moments. "Are you sure?"

"Yeah, unless you're tired. I'd enjoy the company."

She poured herself a cup and chose the seat opposite Rich's. Then an awkward silence fell.

As if both felt the pressure, they spoke at the same time.

"Do you—" Rich began.

"Maybe I—"

"Sorry," Rich added. "I wanted to know if you planned on marrying, having a family."

Sam hadn't expected that question. "I—I'd like to, but it's not likely to happen."

"Why not?"

"I move around a lot. And most men hope for a woman who can bring something to the marriage. Like property, or influence, or something. All I can offer is good table service."

Rich leaned forward. "That's not true! Don't say something like that. You have a lot to offer."

She shrugged her shoulders.

"A man likes a woman he can be proud of. You sure fill that bill. Doyle was practically drooling the other day."

Sam shook her head, smiling a little. "And Doyle's so selective?"

Rich grinned. "Maybe not, but Jim is, I can assure you."

Ah, they were back to tonight. "I'm sure Jim was teasing."

"Yeah, he was, because we've got a hard-and-fast rule about each other's women."

"That must make life difficult for your cousins," she said, lifting her chin.

"What do you mean?" he asked, frowning.

"There can't be many women in the county that you haven't dated, from what I've heard."

"Hey! That's not true. I have a reputation, but most of it isn't accurate," he assured her.

"Right. I think I'll go on to bed, Rich. It's late."

"Wait! Are you happy here?"

She wondered what he was really asking. "Yes, of course. Lavinia is wonderful."

"And me?"

"Ah. You're wanting to know what I'll say to your father? Don't worry, Rich. If he asks, I'll tell your father you've been very helpful."

"And our kisses?"

She didn't want to talk about those moments, ones that she would treasure. "I don't think that's any of your father's business." She turned to leave, but Rich stood and caught her by the arm.

"In that case," he muttered, pulling her closer, "I think I'll have another one."

Chapter Thirteen

Rich entered the kitchen the next morning and found his grandmother making breakfast. Sam was nowhere in sight.

"Where's Sam? Isn't she going to eat breakfast before church?"

Lavinia kept her head down. "No. Said she had things to do this morning. We're to go to church without her."

"Damn!"

"That's a fine how do you do, cursing on the Lord's day, young man. What's the matter with you?"

"I'm upset, Grandma, that I didn't think of it before."

"You didn't think of cursing before? I've got a better memory than that, child. I even remember threatening to wash your mouth out with soap, so don't—"

"No, not cursing, Grandma. I didn't remember that Sam wouldn't have anything to wear to church. That's why she's not going to church with us. Not because she doesn't want to go."

"You're kidding!" Lavinia stared at him. "That's the reason?"

"I would guess. You saw her entire wardrobe when you went through the duffel bag."

"Mercy, I'd forgotten that. I just assumed— She doesn't own a dress?"

He shook his head. She'd worn jeans last night. In fact, she'd been a little nervous about going to his parents' welcome home party until he told her she needed to talk Lavinia into going. Maybe Sam's nervousness had been because she didn't have anything to wear but blue jeans.

When Lavinia raced past him, he realized he'd goofed again. He didn't want his grandmother making a big deal about Sam's lack of wardrobe. He hurried after, reaching Sam's room right behind her.

"What is it, Lavinia? Is something wrong?" Samantha asked, standing and staring at his grandmother.

"There certainly is! Why didn't you tell me why you turned down my invitation to church?"

"Uh, Grandma, maybe—" Rich began, seeing Sam's cheeks flush in embarrassment.

Both women ignored him. "I'm not used to going to church, Lavinia. Is it a requirement of the job?" Samantha asked quietly.

"No, child, of course not. But Rich said you refused because you don't have a dress to wear."

"That's true. I don't want to embarrass you."

"But I can—" Lavinia began.

"No. I'll find something to wear before next week,

okay? And occasionally I'll go to church with you.''
Sam took Lavinia's hands in hers and squeezed them.

Rich stood there watching Samantha reach out to his
grandmother, anxious to make her happy, and smiled.
He'd finally figured out that Samantha, with all her stiff-
ness and determination, had a soft heart. She would
deny it if Rich said anything, but she did.

"We'll pick you up after church. We're all going
next door for lunch,'' he said, watching her.

"No,'' Sam said calmly, a word she frequently used
with him. "I don't want to intrude on family time.''

Lavinia chuckled. "Intrude? With that bunch? You'll
just be another one of the kids. Abby will be there, you
know. She told me she hoped to spend more time with
you. She likes you.''

"I like her, too, Lavinia, but I don't think— She'll
want to concentrate on Russ.''

Rich cut to the chase. "You look fine. By the time
we get there, everyone will have changed. We might
even go for a ride.''

Her response proved how well he'd understood her.
"You're sure?''

Lavinia stared first at Samantha and then her grandson. "Of course he's sure. Don't expect me to get on a
horse, but you young people will. We'll pick you up at
half past noon.'' Then she leaned forward and kissed
Samantha's cheek.

"Come on down and eat breakfast,'' Rich added.
"Grandma's cooked more food than necessary again.
No reason to let it go to waste.''

Samantha agreed and followed them down the stairs.

"WHERE'S SAM?" Janie whispered to her mother as they sat side by side in the church pew.

"Home. Didn't have anything to wear," Lavinia said briefly in a whisper.

Pete frowned at Janie, and she didn't pursue the conversation until after the sermon ended and everyone began filing out of the church.

"She thought she should dress up? Wear heels, nylons, stuff like that? We're more casual than that," Janie stated.

"You don't get it, child. Neither did I. But to my amazement, Rich did."

"Get what?"

"All she owns is blue jeans. Remember that duffel bag? She has a spare pair of jeans and a couple of T-shirts, and one pair of gym shoes."

"Surely, she has—" Janie began with a frown. Then she stopped. "And Rich understood?"

"Yeah. I love the boy, but I've never thought of him as ultrasensitive. But I may have misjudged him."

"Rich?" Janie called to her son who was several feet ahead of her.

He waited for her at the front door. They both shook the pastor's hand and stepped outside. The day was gloomy, dark clouds were gathering.

"What is it, Mom?"

"How did you know Samantha didn't have anything to wear?"

He shrugged his shoulders. "I guessed. She travels light."

"No woman travels that light!" Janie exclaimed.

"Mom, Samantha doesn't rely on anyone. She keeps to herself and tries to make sure she doesn't owe any favors. She told me she moves around a lot."

Pete returned to his wife's side. Wrapping an arm around her, he asked, "What's wrong, hon?"

Janie grabbed her husband's arm. "Let's go to the truck. I don't want to say anything here."

With a big man on each side, Janie said nothing else until Pete opened the passenger door of his pickup. Then she looked into her husband's face and said, "Pete, Sam couldn't come to church because all she has are blue jeans."

He stared at his wife's beautiful face, seeing tears in her eyes and slowly put her statement together. "That's why she didn't come to church?"

Janie nodded.

"Well, damn!" Pete said as he frowned. "We'll just buy her some new clothes."

Janie exchanged a look with Rich. She knew her husband's heart. When their children needed something, Pete never hesitated to provide it unless Janie fought him, saying their children had to learn to provide for themselves. "You can't do that."

"Now, Janie, I can. You know we have enough money."

"Dad, that's not the problem." Rich said. "*I* have enough money. Grandma has enough money, but Sam refused her offer. She said she'd buy something before next week."

"Damn, I haven't even told her her money's in the bank," Pete replied. "I opened an account for her before we left for Hawaii and Brett should have deposited her salary in there, but I didn't get her to sign the card. I'll get her to do that today and then take it to the bank.''

"Oh, good," Janie exclaimed. "I'll buy her something as a present for taking care of Mom. That's reasonable, and she can buy something if she wants." She beamed at her husband. "That will work."

"I'm not sure it will," Rich said, still looking grim. "She tries to keep her belongings minimal, so she can carry everything. She's pretty disciplined."

This time it was Pete who recognized the problem. "She still doesn't feel like she's part of the family?"

"I think it'll be a while before she feels that way."

After standing there with his hands on his hips, Pete finally looked up. "It's hard to think about not having anyone to turn to. Anyone who understands what you're going through. Who can pitch in when you need help. Someone you can laugh with."

"Yeah," Rich agreed, his voice a little hoarse with emotion. "But she tries to help people, to reach out to them. She wanted Grandma to be happy this morning. That's why she agreed to buy something."

Pete cleared his throat. "Yeah. She's a good girl."

Janie hugged both her men. "We'll fix her up."

"It would help if everyone changes to casual clothes before we come to lunch today. And not say anything about her lack of clothes."

"She's coming to lunch?" Janie asked, pleasure on her face.

"Yeah, Mom, she's coming. I think you love her more than me!" he added with a grin.

"Oh, you!" Janie exclaimed. "I'm just looking forward to taking Sam on a shopping trip. Anna, Megan and B.J. all have daughters to share with, but now I have someone to shop for."

She climbed into the truck, beaming now, and Pete closed the door. "It's a woman thing. I hope Sam doesn't mind."

"As long as Mom offers because she wants to reward her for taking care of Grandma, I think she'll be okay." Rich hoped that was true. He was beginning to realize how difficult life was for Sam. He wanted her to be happy.

SAMANTHA WAS neatly dressed in jeans and her blue T-shirt. Nearby was the jean jacket that had been her only coat. If she stayed until next winter— She broke off that thought. She hadn't remained more than six months anywhere since her father died. She couldn't think that far ahead.

Lavinia might not need a housekeeper much longer. It was clear to Samantha that a little attention and involvement in what was going on around her had made a big difference. And Samantha had some ideas for Lavinia's future.

When Abby had been there last weekend, she'd expressed envy that Sam was learning to knit. Lavinia had offered to teach both of them how to crochet, too. Samantha decided there might be other young women who'd be interested. If they offered a class a couple of nights a week, it might be a good thing.

She wanted to talk to Abby about it, but she didn't think she should propose the idea herself. But Abby might agree. Now, she'd get to visit with Abby today.

She wasn't sure she could stay much longer for another reason. Rich's kiss last night had been as wonderful as the others, but it only made her want more. It wasn't that Rich wouldn't cooperate. He had initiated the kiss last night. The problem was she didn't want to stop at just kissing.

Rich would insist on marriage if they took things further. Not because he wanted to marry but because he'd believe he'd have to. So if she invited him to make love to her, she knew she'd have to leave at once.

She'd love to stay here all her life, married to Rich. But having come to realize that she might be falling for him, she knew she couldn't marry him when he didn't love her. So, if she made the choice to sleep with Rich, she'd be back on the road soon after.

She heard Lavinia's car driving down the dirt road. Quickly she checked her long braid to be sure her hair was tidy. And prayed that Rich was right about everyone being casual, maybe going for a ride. She wanted to blend in.

She'd used the time they were gone to scrub the kitchen, leaving enough time for a quick shower. She didn't want Lavinia to think she'd slept the morning away.

Now she stepped to the door and opened it. ''Morning. Are you coming in, or should I come out?''

"I need to collect some things I told Mildred I'd bring her," Lavinia said as she slipped from behind the wheel. "She and I are making a quilt for Russ and Abby's wedding present."

"Oh, how wonderful, Lavinia. What a terrific idea!"

"You think so? Good. I'll show you what I've gotten done."

She kissed Samantha's cheek as she hurried past her. Rich slowly followed his grandmother.

"Do you do it on purpose?" he asked as he approached her.

Her eyes widened as she stared at him. "Do what on purpose?"

"Make her feel good."

Samantha stepped back, frowning. "I don't understand."

"Do you tell her what she does is wonderful because it will make her feel good, or because you really mean it?"

"Because I really mean it! How could you think— A homemade quilt is a rare thing. Why, people pay as much as five hundred dollars for one of those. And to have it made by her husband's two grandmothers... That is something you can pass down to your children! Anyone who didn't appreciate that would be an idiot!" She glared at him.

He chuckled. "That's what I thought. How did you figure all that out when you never had a mother? When you've been alone for so long?"

She continued to glare at him. "Because I'm not an

diot. I do okay, but I know what I'm missing! You need to appreciate your family more.''

Her assumption that he didn't appreciate his family irritated him. ''I do appreciate them.''

She turned her back on him and walked into the kitchen. He followed her, grabbing her arm to turn her to face him again. He stared into her green eyes, wondering what was eating her. ''I love my family.''

''Like that's hard,'' she muttered.

''Listen, lady, I'm not stupid. I know they're great, but it's not always fun to have so many people keeping an eye on you. It's not even just family. The entire community watched us grow up.''

''Poor you,'' she said with mock sympathy.

He knew she'd had a hard life. He knew it. But he didn't like her attitude. His grandmother already loved her. She should appreciate that more. He opened his mouth to tell her she was lucky and she, at the same time, jerked her arm from his grasp.

It wasn't a conscious choice, he realized later. He pulled her back around and pressed her against his chest and lowered his lips to hers. And discovered that the magic he'd felt every time he kissed her had multiplied.

To his surprise, her arms went around his neck. As if she liked him kissing her. That boggled his mind. Even last night she'd initially resisted him. But not today. He knew he was wrong to keep kissing her, but she was addictive. He liked what was happening. It was lust, of course.

Any man could understand lust. He'd been without a woman a long time. She shifted, and he drew her closer, between his legs. Imagining that they would reach the obvious conclusion of the kiss.

His hands began to roam her body, even touching her breasts through the T-shirt. The desire to sweep that material from her body, providing him with even more stimulation, was already moving him to catch the hem of her shirt and push it upward.

"Rich!" his grandmother said.

Rich dropped his arms from Samantha's body and opened his eyes.

The shock in Sam's green eyes reminded him of his inappropriate behavior. He was going to have to tell his dad he could never think of Sam as his sister. Never.

"Sorry." He backed away. "Sorry," he repeated.

Samantha continued to stare at him, her arms hanging numbly down her sides. He remembered the softness of them around his neck. He wanted them there again.

Lavinia coughed. "Well, are we ready to go?"

Rich stared at her, his mind not processing what she'd said. "Go?"

"To lunch, boy. We're going to get to the main house and have nothing to eat because of all those healthy appetites over there. Let's go."

Rich backed away and waved the women in front of him. "Yeah, sure."

His gaze followed Samantha as she walked out the kitchen, ignoring him. He'd swear she'd enjoyed that kiss. He was sure of that. But she wasn't acting like she had. That irritated him.

Didn't she think he was a good enough kisser? He hadn't had any complaints before. Maybe he should give it more effort. If they'd been alone, he would've demanded to know why she was acting like a store mannequin. Why her soft breasts were so clearly outlined by her T-shirt. Why her lips were so—so soft, yet hungry.

Why her body fit so perfectly to his?

Why he couldn't think straight?

SAMANTHA BLINDLY followed Lavinia out the doorway of the house. She couldn't quite remember where they were going. But she was sure Lavinia could be trusted.

Neither she nor Rich were in that category. He clearly couldn't be trusted to keep his hands to himself. She couldn't be trusted to protect herself. While his parents had been gone, he'd treated her as a friend. It had been a heady experience. One she liked. They'd worked well together.

But that kiss, that incredible kiss, meant things might be about to change.

"Do you want to drive, Samantha?" Lavinia asked.

"Uh, no, I'll sit in the back seat."

Lavinia got behind the wheel. "When will your cast come off, Rich? I like it when you drive," she said, looking at her grandson.

"I have an appointment with Doc tomorrow. He'll x-ray my ankle and then decide."

Sam was amazed that the man could talk normally. Obviously the kiss hadn't meant anything to him. He was probably just like some other cowboys she'd known, willing to take his pleasures where he found them.

Maybe he wasn't affected by that kiss. Maybe his heart was cold, his body unresponsive. She shook her head, hoping she could put that kiss aside. Discovering the magic of two bodies wasn't something she needed to do. Feeling that emotion she'd found when he touched her wasn't a good thing. She'd promised herself she'd remain alone.

There had been plenty of cowboys who had offered to initiate her in the ways of love. But she'd known it wasn't love they were interested in. Just lust. Because she'd never have any future with any of them. They'd sleep with her, but they wouldn't marry her. She'd always be alone.

"We're here," Lavinia said, her gaze on Samantha in the rearview mirror.

"Oh! Yes. We are. I'm starving," she said. Then she realized how Rich could translate those words and blushed. She hurried out of the car. Abby shouted a greeting to Sam and she hurried to her like a drowning man trying to get to shore.

Lavinia sat in the car, her lips pressed tightly together. She said to Rich, "If she leaves, I'm holding you to blame, young man. Make sure she doesn't." Then she got out of the car.

Rich's door opened and Toby grinned at him. "Thinking about leaving, Rich?" When Rich didn't respond, he leaned in the door. "Rich? Are you all right?"

"I don't know," he said, trying to think about what he was going to do to make sure Sam didn't leave.

"Want me to get Pete?" Toby asked.

''No! No, I'm fine. I—I have some thinking to do, that's all.''

''Okay, come on in. The dinner is ready and it smells good, as usual.''

Rich had an appetite, all right. But it wasn't for whatever Red and Mildred had prepared. He wanted to kiss Samantha again.

But he couldn't.

Not because she might not let him. Her arms around his neck told him she might kiss him back. But his grandmother was right. It was possible Samantha would walk away. It seemed to be a pattern she'd followed all her life. If things got too complicated, she moved on.

How would he face his parents or his grandmother if his hunger for Samantha drove her away?

How would he face himself?

Chapter Fourteen

Much to Samantha's surprise, she enjoyed her afternoon at the Randall ranch. They didn't go riding, as Rich had suggested. Because of the dreary weather, they stayed inside.

Pete gave her a checkbook after lunch, drawing her to one side and asking her to sign the card that would go on file. Afraid he was offering her charity, she gathered her strength to refuse him. But, she discovered instead, that he was paying her her salary.

"Pete, this is too much. Living with Lavinia isn't tough work. I've worked a lot harder for less than half this amount, and it didn't include room and board."

"Don't say that to Janie. She thinks you've worked a miracle."

Sam stared at Pete, confused. "What miracle?"

"You probably haven't noticed, but Lavinia was fading away, giving up interest in life, until you came along. Look at her," he added, nodding in Lavinia's direction. "She's been talking nonstop with Mildred since she got here."

"That's not because of me. That's because they're

making a quilt, she and Mildred, for Abby and Russ. Isn't that a wonderful idea?''

"Yeah, honey, it's great. But you've done your share, too. Janie's going to ask you to go shopping with her because she wants to buy you a special gift for making it possible for her to go to Hawaii. Don't turn her down. She's felt slighted because she didn't have a girl to shop for. She's the only one in the family without a daughter. Now, she's so excited she can hardly think of anything else.''

"But, Pete, she doesn't have to—"

"One lousy shopping trip, Sam. That won't hurt too much, will it?" Pete asked her with a grin. "I admit, it sounds like torture to me, but it means a lot to Janie.''

Samantha struggled with all the different issues, but finally she said, "I don't want to make Janie unhappy.''

"Good choice. I never want Janie to be unhappy.''

Samantha patted his arm. "I know. That's one of the special things about you, Pete.''

He chuckled. "Not special. Just smart. Did anyone ever tell you about my courting Janie?''

"A little.''

"I made Janie unhappy. Before we resolved our problem, half the family was upset. Chad and Megan had just married, but he found himself sleeping on a sofa. So did Hank, Lavinia's husband. I'm not a slow learner. Now I make sure Janie is happy.''

They both laughed together, but Samantha had known Pete for a good number of years. She'd noticed that he didn't mess around with any of the women who hung around the rodeos. Instead he had befriended her, a bedraggled waif. He'd even brought her a stuffed bunny rabbit that she'd carried with her everywhere until it fell apart. Whatever excuses he gave for protecting Janie, Sam knew it was because he was a good man.

"Now," Pete said with a grin, "it's the kids who have to do cleanup while us senior citizens put up our feet. So you'd best get over there and pitch in."

She saw the young people, even Rich, clearing the table and gasped. She didn't want to be thought to be shirking work.

"'Bout time you pitched in," Rich said in a teasing voice. Several others protested, saying she was a guest.

"Guest, hell! She's part of the family now. Besides, she ate, didn't she? That's reason enough to join the cleaning."

Abby threw a wet dishcloth at him, hitting him in the face and he lunged at her, the cloth in his hand.

Elizabeth, Toby's wife, protested. "I think you're just trying to get out of wiping the table. Get to work!"

In the midst of all the teasing and laughter, Samantha found herself relaxing, feeling like part of a family more than she ever had.

"Is it always this much fun!" she whispered to Abby as she dried dishes alongside her.

"Amazing, isn't it?" Abby agreed with a grin. "I already knew Elizabeth before Russ and I got engaged, but the sheer number of cousins and the good humor is overwhelming at first. Not that they're always happy. Sometimes they get into arguments. But they're all good people. I feel very lucky."

"Is everyone here today?"

"No, and Tori, Jim and a couple of others will leave in a few minutes to go back to college. Most summers they're all here. Except Caroline. She's in medical school in Chicago. Tori will graduate this spring and be home. I don't know what she's going to do with her life though. You met her the other night, didn't you?"

"Yes, I like her very much. She doesn't look like the rest of the Randalls. I hope I didn't offend her when I told her that."

Just then Tori walked by carrying several dried platters. Abby said, "Tori, when are you leaving?"

"In a few minutes. Sam, I hope you'll be here when I come back. It's nice to have more people here who aren't real Randalls." With a laugh, she added, "Makes me feel more normal."

"I— Maybe I will be."

"It will be quiet until all of you come home since Casey is the only one still in high school," Abby said.

"He's sweet," Sam said.

"Yeah, there's not a bad one in the bunch. It's amazing. Of course, I'm prejudiced, but I think Russ is one of the best." Abby chuckled. "But don't tell him I said that."

Rich must've been listening because he leaned close to Abby and said, "Don't you think he's figured it out by now since you make calf eyes at him all the time?"

Abby fussed at her future brother-in-law, but Sam knew she didn't care about Rich's teasing.

The kitchen was quickly cleaned, with all the workers, and Samantha was worrying about what would happen next. Just as they finished, Janie came into the kitchen, along with the other mothers and chased the guys away.

Janie ordered Elizabeth, Abby and Samantha to join them at the table for a planning meeting.

"Planning for what?" Elizabeth asked.

"Shopping!" Janie exclaimed, beaming.

The other ladies asked questions and showed pleasure in response. Samantha remained quiet. Surely this wasn't what Pete meant? A big shopping trip? She'd figured she and Janie would go to that small store in Rawhide and spend half an hour choosing something simple.

"We wondered if you two, Abby and Elizabeth, could take next Friday off and we could all go to Casper, or, if you want, Denver," B.J. said. "We need to find the bridesmaids gowns for your wedding, Abby. I'll vote as Caroline, Anna will vote for Tori and Jess, and Elizabeth will be able to vote for herself." She grinned at Abby. "And you have veto power."

"Mmm, power. I like the sound of that!" the bride to-be giggled.

"And you, young lady," Janie said, looking at Samantha, "get a present from me for taking such good care of Mom."

"But that would leave Lavinia alone," Samantha protested. "I can stay here—"

"Don't even think it. It's my first time to have a girl to shop for. I'm so looking forward to it."

Every female eye stared at Samantha and she immediately surrendered. She was glad Pete had prepared her, because she knew Janie would persuade her any way. "But I think it's not the first time you've shopped for me," she added. "I don't think Pete picked out the hair ribbons, or my bunny."

"You remember those?" Janie asked, happiness in her eyes. "I hoped you did."

Elizabeth leaned forward. "Uh, I can take Friday off and go, but, well, I'm not going to be in the wedding."

Everyone stared at her, but Abby seemed devastated by her announcement. "Elizabeth! Why not? You're my maid of honor."

"In just a minute you'll understand." She stood and went to the kitchen door. Opening it, she called, "Toby? Now's the time."

Several of the ladies frowned as they heard a lot of male footsteps. The door opened and the men filed in, most of them with curious looks on their faces. Lavinia, Mildred and Red were the last to enter.

Elizabeth took Toby's hand and waited until everyone filled the big kitchen. Then she looked at her husband and nudged him. He put his arm around her shoulders and kissed her. Then he looked at his family. "We have an announcement to make. We're adding to the number of Randalls."

As if he'd detonated a bomb, there were congratulations, screaming, a few tears and a lot of happiness filling the room.

"But why aren't you going to be my maid of honor?" Abby asked, still upset by Elizabeth's earlier announcement.

"Because I wouldn't be able to fit in a bridesmaid

gown by then, Abby. I'll be six months pregnant. I'm already three months along,'' Elizabeth pointed out.

Her mother, Megan, gasped. ''You kept it a secret for three months?''

Elizabeth immediately began explaining to her mother. Since Toby was Jake's adopted son and B.J.'s real son, two parts of the Randall family were sharing this first child of the next generation. Samantha listened as everyone asked questions, discussed the due date and asked about Elizabeth's health.

The pride and excitement on Jake Randall's face reminded her of the stories she'd heard about him marrying off his brothers, only to be caught in the trap himself. But, according to Pete, Jake was one very happy cowboy when he married B.J.

In the midst of all the happiness, Sam also thought about carrying a child in her body. She'd wanted a child, but she knew she couldn't have one. Not and still remain independent. When Rich had asked her if she wanted a family, she'd avoided answering. But the reality was that there was nothing she wanted more. If she had the choice of a family like the Randalls, a support team to be there for her and her baby, she'd be the happiest person in the world. How wonderful for Elizabeth and Toby that they had such family support and love.

But if she got pregnant and was on her own, she'd be petrified she wouldn't be able to take care of her child. She couldn't take that chance, the chance that her child would, like her, be alone.

But she was almost sick to her stomach from the wanting.

Someone touched her shoulder. She looked up to discover Rich standing behind her. "You okay?" he asked softly.

"Yes. It's very exciting, isn't it?"

His participation in the news shone in his brown eyes, but he only said, "I don't know. Babies cry and poop. I'm not sure they're such a bargain."

Samantha turned away, not wanting to share her feelings with Rich. She needed to keep her distance instead of grow closer to him. Besides, she'd be long gone by the time the baby was born.

That thought actually hurt. The temptation to throw herself into the welcome she'd been given, to consider herself at home, was a temptation, a trap, because one day she'd be gone, suffering greater pain than she'd ever known.

Because she was already in love with the sprawling, loving Randall family.

RICH WAS HAPPY for his cousins. Happy that the Randall family was continuing to grow. He supposed Russ and Abby would be the next parents. But he couldn't see himself in that position, building a family. A flash of Samantha, holding a dark-haired baby in her arms, startled him.

Whoa! What was going on? He wasn't going to— Samantha was a loner. They had no future together. He was attracted to her, of course, but when he'd asked her about a future, she hadn't acted as if she wanted one with him.

He looked at Toby, remembering everyone's surprise when he declared his love for Elizabeth. Even though they shared no common blood, they'd been raised as cousins. Toby must've had a hard time letting Elizabeth know his feelings. Fortunately, she seemed to have followed the same path.

He looked at Samantha again. What was she thinking? Did that kiss this morning cross her mind? He'd talk to her this evening. Let her know she had nothing to worry about. He'd keep his hands to himself. Since that seemed to be what she wanted. Damn it!

Mildred and Lavinia stood and started taking down glasses to fix everyone a drink so they could make a toast to the new baby due next October. Samantha got up to help them and bumped into Rich. Shivers rushed through him and he realized not touching Samantha was going to take a lot of control. But he could do it. Of course he could.

Soon, everyone had a glass and Jake lifted his. "To the growth of the Randalls. And to this special child, due in October, the month my first son and I already share."

It hadn't occurred to Rich that Toby and Jake shared an October birthday. It would be amazing if the baby was born on their special day. Almost as if Toby becoming a Randall had been preordained. He shivered again, as if someone was walking over his grave. Had the same thing happened to him and Samantha? He just happened to be in the restaurant where she worked. Just happened to have a broken ankle and need help.

And she just happened to need to get away.

His grandmother just happened to need company.

He just happened to kiss her.

Had events already been set in motion? Was he destined to fulfill that picture he'd earlier seen of Samantha?

"No!" he growled in a pause of conversation so that everyone hear his exclamation.

"No, what?" Jake asked. "You don't want the baby to be born in October?" He seemed highly offended.

"No, of course not, Uncle Jake. I think that would be great. I was thinking about, uh, something else."

"Well, focus, boy. We've got some celebrating to do."

Chad raised his glass. "Yeah, Jake and I are going to be grandpas!" He suddenly stopped smiling. "Wait a minute. That means people will think I'm old!"

"How do you think I feel?" Red asked. "I'm going to be a great-grandfather!" He raised his glass. "Well, I'll tell you how I feel. I'm powerful glad to have that title!"

ON THE WAY HOME, Samantha had a lot to think about. It seemed the shopping trip to Denver was still on. Abby convinced Elizabeth to still be her maid of honor, certain they could find a dress that would look just right for her as her pregnancy progressed.

Samantha was more excited than anyone. With the money she'd earned, she could do some shopping, too.

It sounded like so much fun, shopping with friends. She'd never done that before. Of course, when she had to leave, she might have to leave some things behind, but she'd enjoy them while she could.

And Elizabeth and Toby's baby. Oh, how she wanted to stay until the baby was born. She made a silent plea that she'd be able to stay that long. Then she'd leave. But already she was picturing the different stages of growth for the baby and knew she'd want to be here for each one. She'd definitely better plan on leaving before the baby's birth.

Suddenly the excitement went out of her. She had to leave, and she knew it. Buying clothes would be a waste of time. She was fortunate she'd gotten to stay until her arm and shoulder had recovered. She wouldn't have been able to get a waitressing job while she was hurt.

But she had to leave, even if she hadn't been well. Because of Rich. He was a good man. And an incredible kisser. She wouldn't be able to resist him. Or what he would offer because he had to if they— Yes, she definitely would have to leave.

No future here. Not even for a few months. She'd been fooling herself. The thought of going through the summer, with picnics, rides, sharing their thoughts and feelings with each other… Samantha knew she was too weak to resist Rich's touch. And the moment she did give in to what she wanted, everything would be ruined.

She already knew him well. He might think he was going to remain single for years, but she figured he'd marry soon. He and Russ had spent too many years sharing life. Now that Russ had Abby, Rich would find someone. Someone he respected and loved, she hoped.

Not someone he'd been forced to marry.

Maybe she should go before next Friday. Before she wasted her money on things she couldn't take with her. Before she thought too much about leaving. Before she weakened.

Lavinia parked the car in front of her house. "That was fun today, but it's good to be home."

"Yeah," Rich agreed, reaching for his door handle. "Lots of excitement."

"I reckon Russ and Abby will be next, and I'll be Great-Grandma. You'd better start looking for your own lady, Rich, or your brother's going to pass you by."

"It's not a race, Grandma," Rich admonished. "I have to find the right lady. Someone who wants the same things." Then he opened the door and got out.

Samantha, with her head down, followed him. It occurred to her that Rich had everything any woman could want. So it shouldn't take much time for him to find his match, if he ever started looking.

Good thing she'd already decided to leave. She was coming to realize how much it would hurt for him to bring his future bride to Lavinia's. She'd have to leave then, for sure. But she wouldn't be able to resist temptation that long. She was sure about that.

"Help Samantha with those leftovers, will you, Rich? Red and Mildred sent enough food for supper tonight. No need to do any cooking."

After they got the food into the house, Sam ran upstairs. When she came down a few minutes later, Rich and his grandmother were quietly talking in the kitchen. He looked up when she entered.

"Sam, I need to check on a mare in the barn. She's due any time. Could you come with me and hold the flashlight?"

"There are lights in the barn," she said in surprise. "Why do you need—"

"The overheads are dim. I'm going to need more light to examine her."

"Will B.J. be coming over?" Since his aunt was an experienced vet, it seemed Rich should call her.

"Maybe, once I check the mare out. I don't want to make B.J. drive out if it isn't necessary."

"Go help him, please, dear. He's promised to be good." Lavinia added a smile to her request.

Samantha's cheeks flushed and she abruptly agreed. "Sure. Where's the flashlight?" She would do almost anything Lavinia asked of her.

"You'd better get your jacket," Rich told her. "It still gets cold at night."

She got her jean jacket and returned to the kitchen. Grandmother and grandson were talking quietly again, as if they were sharing a secret.

After watching in suspicion, she cleared her throat. "I'm ready."

"Good," Lavinia said, smiling again. "I'll take a little nap while you two work."

Rich said nothing, just led the way out of the kitchen. When she stepped out onto the porch, she realized the sun had disappeared behind the mountains since they'd gotten home. The stars filled the night sky, and a full moon offered enough light to find their way to the barn.

"What do you do in the winter? If it snows, how do you get to the barns?" she asked, looking for a distraction. She was getting very nervous about their trip to the barn.

"We use the rope system. It's easy to get lost in a blizzard. So we connect ropes between the barns and the house and bunkhouse."

"Oh."

"Don't worry, we won't let you get lost," he said with a laugh.

She said nothing, knowing she wouldn't be there for the July wedding, much less the winter storms. She blinked her eyes, to dismiss the tears. She couldn't understand why she was having trouble with tears. She seldom cried. She'd learned the hard way that tears helped nothing. In fact, it made men think she was weak, easy prey.

She mustn't let Rich think she was weak.

There was no more conversation until Rich shoved back the big door of the barn. He flicked on a light and Samantha didn't think it was too weak. But she'd admit she hadn't examined a pregnant horse before.

"I'll get the flashlight," Rich said and strode down the row of stalls toward the tack room.

Her tension lessened somewhat. He hadn't jumped her, tried to resume what they'd started in the kitchen that morning, so maybe his request was legitimate. She hoped so. She wouldn't be able to resist that pleasure, she feared.

Rich came out of the tack room and motioned her forward to a stall halfway down the barn. The mare in that stall was standing, looking miserable with her head down, her stomach large. Even Samantha knew she was near her time.

"Is she all right?"

"That's what we're going to find out," Rich assured her. "Dixie, here, is a first-time mom."

"Oh, poor baby." She patted the horse's nose and neck.

"She's an Appaloosa. I'm hoping her baby has the markings, too." He began examining the horse.

Samantha stepped forward and pointed the light in the proper direction.

When Rich finished, he patted the horse on her rump and stepped back. Samantha turned off the flashlight and handed it to him as she asked, "Is Dixie all right?"

"Yeah. I think maybe we've got a couple of more days, yet."

A couple of days. She might not be able to stay until Elizabeth's baby was born, but maybe she could see Dixie's baby into the world.

Pleasure poured through her.

But Rich's next words immediately wiped the pleasure away.

"Sam, I lied to you."

Chapter Fifteen

When Samantha began backing away, Rich figured he'd blown it already. "Whoa, Sam! Let me explain."

She stopped, and he figured it was the first time she'd done as he asked. "I didn't lie about anything so bad. I just didn't need you to come out to the barn with the flashlight."

She stared at him. Then she asked, "Is that it?"

"Yeah."

"Why did you ask me out here, then?"

"Because I wanted to apologize to you without Grandma hearing us." He ducked his head in embarrassment.

"Apologize for what?"

He snapped his head up and stared at her. "This morning."

She didn't say anything. But she didn't look at him either.

"Sam, I know kissing you was— I should've asked you—" He cleared his throat. "Uh, I'm really attracted to you. If you were someone I'd known for a while, we could, you know, take it easy. But I don't want to stop when we—you know. So it's best if we don't start.''

"I—I didn't exactly push you away.''

"Yeah,'' he said. What she said was true, but that didn't take away his blame. "It's still my fault. I just wanted to tell you I'm going to try real hard not to touch you anymore. I think it's some kind of chemical reaction. Nothing to be done but avoid each other.''

"Yes, there's something to do. I need to leave.''

She turned to walk out of the barn, but Rich couldn't let her leave. He hurried around her to lean against the closed barn door.

"Now, Sam, you can't do that.''

"Why not? I only promised to be here a week.''

"You can't do that because Grandma loves you. I don't want her hurt.''

"She'll forget me in a while. Abby's going to arrange some things for Lavinia that will help.'' She edged to his side, but he put out an arm to stop her.

"What things?''

"We're— I mean, Abby is going to get Lavinia to teach a class at night to young ladies. How to knit and crochet. Maybe even demonstrate quilting. As long as she's needed and has lots to do, she'll be all right.''

"That's a good plan, Sam. Thanks.''

"Abby's doing it.''

"Because you thought of it.'' She was close enough to touch. He'd really like to hold her in his arms again. To have her hold him. She was right. It was nice to feel needed.

"I need to go in and get some rest." She avoided his gaze.

"First you need to promise me you won't run away. Dad and Mom would be upset, too."

"Rich, you don't understand. I don't fit into this family. I never will. I'm a loner. I move around. We scarcely speak the same language. I left school in middle school. All of you have degrees."

"But you talk like you're educated," he pointed out. "Why is that?"

She dropped her head. "I spent a lot of time in libraries when I was younger. I read a lot. The librarians helped me."

He pictured her sitting in a chair too big for her, reading books because she had nowhere to go. "Good for you. You probably know a lot more than me."

She shook her head. "I have to go. Lavinia's probably fixing dinner."

"She'll wait on us. She knows I'm apologizing. She said she'd hold me responsible if you went away." He tried a smile but it didn't seem to affect her.

"I can't promise what's going to happen in the future, Rich."

"Okay, promise you won't run away tonight. Can you do that? Can you promise that I'll see you at breakfast tomorrow?"

She sighed. "Okay, fine, I won't run away tonight."

"Whew! Thank you, now we can go to the house. I don't think Grandma intended to let me eat if I didn't get your promise." This time he smiled big, hoping she'd at least smile a little.

But he'd made the mistake of relaxing his arms, and she slipped past him. He caught up with her after turning out the light and closing the door. But she didn't respond to his teasing.

Lavinia met them at the back door. "Everything okay?"

This time Samantha reached out and kissed Lavinia's cheek. "Of course. I'm starving."

"Me, too," Rich agreed and hugged his grandma.

"Good. We'll need to heat things up, son, if you have some work to do."

Ignoring Lavinia's questioning gaze, Samantha moved to the sink to wash her hands. She didn't want to answer any questions right now.

SAMANTHA LAY IN BED as late as possible the next morning. It had taken her a long time to get to sleep. She had plans to make. And dilemmas to solve.

She believed what she'd told Rich. She didn't belong in the Randall family. She had to leave. But she didn't want to leave without more from Rich. She'd decided that she was going to ask him to make love to her.

Not to trap him into marriage. She would leave immediately afterward. But she'd waited all her life for the feelings she experienced when Rich touched her. She was tired of waiting. It would be a sort of reward. It wouldn't hurt Rich. Most men didn't complain about making love. It wouldn't stop him from waiting until the right woman came along.

But she would have memories, wonderful memories, of sharing such intimacy with the one man she'd found who made her feel special when he touched her. She couldn't have a future with him, but she could have her memories.

Responsibly, of course. She couldn't travel pregnant. She couldn't properly provide for a baby. But she could have memories of making love to a man she respected and…cared about.

So she hoped to stay for Dixie's big moment…and her own.

Then she'd go back out into the world and look for another job, another temporary place to live. But she'd have her memories to take with her.

She had a lot to do today.

Breakfast with Rich and Lavinia was good. She watched their expressions, listened to their gentle teasing, stored up the scents of breakfast.

"I need to run into town this morning, Lavinia. Is there anything I can do for you?" she asked. It was the first time she'd asked to go somewhere and both Lavinia and Rich looked surprised.

"Why, no, dear, but you can take Rich to see Doc. I was going to drive him in, but I'm a little tired from our big day yesterday."

"Don't you feel good?" she asked, frowning with concern.

"Sure. I'm just being lazy. When's your appointment, Rich?"

"At eight. Doc said he'd get to me early so I can get some work done."

"Well, mercy, you two had better hurry," Lavinia warned, checking her watch. "It's seven-thirty now."

Sam stood and began clearing off the table.

"Oh, leave that to me, child. I don't have to be anywhere. I'll do it after you're gone."

Sam ignored her and filled one sink with hot, soapy water. Then she filled the water with dirty dishes.

"You stubborn child. You remind me of Janie. And me."

Lavinia looked at Rich. "Tell your father we're going to need that highfalutin dishwasher, now. I don't want that child to get dishpan hands."

"I'll tell him, Grandma."

After they were in the car, Samantha driving, Rich chuckled. "I'm beginning to agree with Mom. You're a miracle worker."

"What are you talking about?"

"Dad has tried many a time to get Grandma to update her kitchen. She's always refused. Now she's changed her mind because she doesn't want you to get dishpan hands."

"I think that's sweet."

"Definitely," Rich agreed.

Nothing more was said until she parked in front of the clinic. "I'll go run my errands and come back and pick you up," she said, ignoring his curious gaze.

"Or you could come in with me and then I'd help you run your errands."

"No, thank you. They're personal."

Fortunately, she knew Doc would take at least half an hour to examine Rich and remove the cast. That should give her enough time, because she didn't trust Rich not to follow her.

The bank was just across the street and the drugstore two doors down. She wouldn't even have to move the car.

In the bank, she withdrew all but fifty dollars of the salary she'd been paid. She didn't close the account because she figured they might call Pete and tell him. Rawhide was a small, personal town.

"You want it all in cash?" the bank teller asked, her voice rising in surprise.

"Yes, please, I'm going on a big shopping spree."

"My goodness, that should be fun," the woman said, smiling.

Her kindness made Sam feel bad. She shouldn't have lied, but she had no choice.

At the drugstore, she bought a small box of condoms, hoping no one would recognize her. She didn't want rumors to start and embarrass the Randalls after she left.

Her last stop was to the feed and general store where the Greyhound bus made a stop every other day. The young woman behind the counter sold her a ticket for Thursday on a bus that would take her to Denver.

When she got back to the clinic, her secrets hidden in her handbag, Rich was waiting. He wiggled his bare foot at her, grinning. "Look! I'm not a cripple anymore."

"Congratulations!" she said. Another memory she'd have. "Ready to go?"

"Doc wanted you to step inside when you got here. He wants to be sure you're healed."

"Oh, there's no need to bother him," she said, backing toward the door.

Rich stood and took her arm. "We all do what Doc says. We're lucky to have him." He pushed open the door beside the little desk and hollered, "Doc, she's here."

The elderly man came out at once. "Hi, there, Sam. How's that arm and shoulder?"

"Just fine, Dr. Jacoby. I'm fine. I didn't mean to bother you."

"No bother. May I?" he asked as he lifted the arm of the T-shirt and peered under it. After Samantha nodded, he slid his hand to her shoulder and rotated it a little. Sam made sure she didn't grimace, even if there still was a little pain.

"All right. Good as new. I'm glad I put in those stitches that disintegrate. Hardly left a scar. You take care now," Doc said cheerfully.

"I will, thank you." She liked the doctor, but she knew she wouldn't be seeing him again.

When they returned to the sidewalk where they parted less than an hour ago, Rich asked, "Did you get all your errands run?"

"Yes, thank you. I'm ready to go back to the ranch."

"I need to go to the drugstore. I ran out of aftershave this morning. Come on, it's a good little store."

Sam stared at him. She couldn't go into the drugstore now, with Rich. The salesgirl might link her purchase to Rich.

"I'm a little pooped, Rich. I think I'll sit in the car while you go in."

"Don't want to be seen with me?" he asked, his eyebrows raised.

"Yes, that's it. I'm afraid my standing in the community will scrape bottom if I'm seen with you." She smiled at him and got in the car.

He gave her a strange look before crossing the street and disappearing into the store.

After five minutes, he returned. "Anything you need?" he asked again, but she refused. Before she could start the engine, he said, "Well, I need something."

Surprised, she stared at him. "What?"

"A cup of coffee. Park by the café."

"Can't you wait until we get home? I'm sure Lavinia will have a pot on."

"Nope. I can't wait."

She did as he asked, but she didn't understand his insistence.

Inside, he waved at the waitress and led her to a booth nearby. "Hi, Mona. We need some coffee."

"I'll be right there, Rich."

Samantha stared at the woman, wondering if she'd been one of Rich's conquests. When she brought over a pot of coffee and two mugs, Sam realized the woman was older than she looked.

"Hi, there. You're the young lady living with Lavinia? How's she doing?"

"Very well, thank you. I'm Samantha Jeffers."

"I'm Mona Woodruff. Keep your eye on this rascal. I baby-sat him a few times."

"Now, Mona, don't start telling those stories about me and Russ running around without our diapers," Rich protested. His cheeks actually reddened.

Samantha couldn't hold back a chuckle. "That doesn't surprise me."

"No, ma'am, no modesty at all," Mona agreed with a grin. "Can I get you anything else? The cinnamon buns are really good today."

"That's what you always say," Rich complained.

"And am I ever wrong?"

"Nope. Bring me one. How about you, Sam?"

"No, thank you. I've been gaining weight ever since I moved in with Lavinia. My jeans are too tight."

"I know what you mean. Lavinia's a good cook," Mona agreed.

"Well, as the only male present, let me go on record as saying I don't object to tight jeans," Rich assured Samantha, raising his eyebrows at her.

"Oh, you!" Mona spoke, swiping him with a towel. "I'd better go get that cinnamon bun before the boss yells at me."

"She's nice," Sam said, looking around the café.

"You could've been working with her. They've got a sign in the window for help wanted." He watched her as if he thought she'd leap at the opportunity.

"It would've been nice. Maybe in a few weeks. I don't think Lavinia really needs help anymore."

"But I think she'll want you around anyway."

Sam shrugged her shoulders.

"Are you looking forward to the shopping trip at the end of the week?"

"Of course." She must not have put enough enthusiasm in her voice because Rich looked skeptical.

"Most ladies like the opportunity to shop," Rich announced as he lifted his cup for a sip. "In fact, most ladies wouldn't be satisfied with Rawhide. Maybe you should've waited until Friday to make your purchases today."

She knew he was fishing about any purchases she might've made. "No, they had everything I needed today."

"Will you enjoy the big shopping expedition?"

"Anyone would enjoy shopping with their friends." Sam chose her words carefully.

"Hmm, maybe I should accompany you on the trip. Elizabeth and Toby did a shopping trip in Denver. Russ went with them, he and Abby."

"I don't think Janie will want you along."

"I'm beginning to feel unloved."

"Right," Samantha said with a grin, knowing Rich was joking. Or at least she hoped he was.

Mona brought out the promised cinnamon bun, and Sam's mouth watered. "Oh, my. I bet those are really good."

"Want me to bring you one?" the waitress asked.

"No, and don't ask again in case I weaken."

Mona grinned and headed for another table.

"You've got great discipline, Sam. A lot better than mine," Rich assured her.

"The longer I stay here, the more it weakens. I'm going to be lonely when I leave here." When she realized what she'd said, she peeked at Rich.

"So, I have a solution. Don't leave."

"Ah. That's an interesting idea." She hoped that remark would satisfy him.

"Here."

She looked up to see him holding out his fork, offering her a bite of cinnamon bun. "No, really, I don't want any."

"You have to taste it, Sam." He held the bite a little closer.

Her resolve disappeared and she leaned across the table and nipped the roll off the fork. It was heavenly, she decided as she closed her eyes to enjoy it.

"Aha! I knew it!" Mona exclaimed.

When Sam opened her eyes, she discovered the waitress staring at her. With a half smile, she said, "I couldn't resist."

"Oh, it's not that, honey," Mona assured her with a big smile. "Couples come in here all the time. But when they start feeding each other, that means they're going to get married! We've been right every time, haven't we, Rich?"

"I haven't kept track, Mona," Rich said calmly.

"Well, I have, so you might as well pick out your wedding dress, young lady. You're church-bound!" she announced to everyone in the café.

"Let's get out of here," Sam urged.

WHEN SAM GOT HOME, Lavinia told her to call Abby. Hurrying to the phone, she discovered Abby had the news she'd been hoping for. At lunch, Sam told Lavinia about her plan for her, and Mildred, too, if she wanted, to teach the young women of the town to knit, crochet and quilt.

"Do you think anyone will come?" Lavinia asked, her gaze fixed on the calendar on the wall.

"Abby thinks so. She'll be there. And I'm sure there are others, too. When Tori comes home, she'll sign up. She told me she wanted to learn to knit. Their own mothers may not know those skills, or have time to teach them. Everyone's so busy these days."

"That's true."

"They're offering a lot of night classes at the high school for adults. Some classes are about reading or accounting, doing your own taxes, and such. But others will be fun activities. And they'll have free baby-sitting."

"It might work. What a good idea. We could even form a quilting circle for us experienced ones. We could make a quilt and auction it off for charity."

"That's wonderful, Lavinia. Talk to Abby about that."

Lavinia nodded. Then she reached across the table to take Samantha's hand. "Thank you, honey."

"Thank Abby."

"I'm going to call Mildred," Lavinia said with more enthusiasm than she'd shown in a while.

Samantha began a marathon cleaning, determined to leave Lavinia's house in perfect condition.

She was scrubbing one of the bathrooms when Lavinia came to find her. "Did Rich tell his dad I want the kitchen redone?"

"I don't think so. He probably forgot. He was excited about getting his cast off."

"Of course. I'll go call Janie now. She'll remember to tell Pete what I want."

"Yes, I'm sure she will."

Before Lavinia returned to the phone, she paused and said, "You're about to scrub the porcelain off that tub. Why don't you take a break? I don't want your arm sore again."

"Doc checked me out today. I'm fine."

Lavinia, her mind on her new kitchen, wandered off.

By suppertime, Samantha was exhausted, but the house shone. She showered before dinner and then came to the kitchen to help Lavinia fix dinner.

When Rich arrived and washed up, the two ladies had a delicious dinner ready for him.

"Man, this looks good. You two are spoiling me," he exclaimed.

Dinner was enjoyable. When it was over, Sam asked about Dixie and if she could accompany Rich to the barn to check on the mare.

"Sure. I'd enjoy the company."

When they stepped outside into the crisp night air, Sam shivered.

"You need a heavier coat, for sure before this winter," Rich said.

She smiled and said nothing.

When they entered the barn and approached Dixie, it was clear the mare was in trouble. Rich hurried into the stall, then ordered Sam to go to the tack room and call B.J. and ask her to come at once.

Samantha hadn't planned on spending her evening in the barn, but she didn't dare leave, afraid she'd miss something. When B.J. arrived, she and Rich worked patiently with the mare to ensure that her foal was born healthy. Samantha watched Rich's strong hands work on the mare. When the foal came out, the mare gave a huge sigh and stood with her head down.

"She won't have any trouble next time, Rich," B.J. assured him. "It's because it's her first. But the filly is a beauty."

"Yes, she is," Rich said. He looked at Sam, hanging over the door of the stall. "Are you okay? It's been a long night."

"But a wonderful one. She's so beautiful."

"A little wobbly, too," he added, smiling at her.

"Babies need help," Sam said softly, thinking of human babies, too. She wanted to have that experience so badly. It was tempting to forget those condoms she'd bought. To take the chance that she might have Rich's child. But that wouldn't be fair to the baby. Or to Rich. She could picture him, helping his child take its first steps. Picking him or her up after a tumble and tears. He'd be a wonderful father, just like Pete.

Tears filled her eyes.

B.J. was cleaning up and Rich joined her at the big sink. Then he hurried to Sam's side. "Are you crying?"

"Not really. Little babies are so sweet. They have no idea— She's trying to nurse!" Sam exclaimed, interrupting her awkward words.

B.J. joined them. "Mother Nature takes over once again. In a day or two, the baby won't wobble at all."

"Amazing."

B.J. looked at her. "It is, isn't it? I'm glad you appreciate the miracle. I've hardly gotten to know you, with all of us milling around.''

''There are a lot of you. But that way you know there'll always be someone to help you if—if anything happens.''

''Yes. Especially when it comes to babies,'' B.J. said with a smile.

Rich surprised Sam by putting his arm around her shoulders in front of his aunt. She'd figured after their visit to the café, he wouldn't be caught close to her no matter what.

''Don't worry,'' he said softly. ''We're not going to let anything happen to this baby, Sam.''

She nodded and smiled. But Rich didn't know about the baby she was thinking about, the one she'd never have.

TWO NIGHTS LATER, she asked Rich to take her down to see the baby filly again. She held her breath when Rich agreed and then asked Lavinia to accompany them. But, much to her relief, Lavinia declined. There was a show on television she wanted to see.

On the walk to the barn, Rich told her how well Dixie and the filly were doing. Then he asked if she wanted to name the foal.

''Me?''

''Yeah, you.''

''Oh, I'd love to. Oh, I know. Let's name her Magnolia! That's a southern flower.''

''Terrific. It's a big name for a little filly, but she'll grow into it. Good choice.''

By that time they'd reached the barn and Rich flipped on the lights. Samantha headed for the stall and reached out to the filly.

Rich came and stood beside her, not touching, but close. After several minutes of praising the animals, he asked, "You ready to go back to the house?"

Samantha took a deep breath. "No, I'm not."

"No? You pet the filly much more and she's going to follow you home," he teased.

"I don't want to pet the filly. I want...I want you to make love to me."

Chapter Sixteen

Rich stared at Samantha, blown away by her re[mark?]
He'd been working so hard to keep everything pl[ain?]
in control. "What did you say?"

Her cheeks were flushed, making him want to [kiss?]
her more than ever. To his surprise, she repeate[d her]
words, not backing down. "I want you to make l[ove to]
me."

When he couldn't think of what to say, she a[sked?]
"Would you mind?"

"Mind? Would I mind? Sam, any man wou[ld be]
thrilled to fulfill your request!"

"Okay." Her answer was calm, as if she'd aske[d him]
to shake hands.

His gaze narrowed. "Why?"

"I think, once we get over the chemistry betwe[en us]
we can relax and life won't be so difficult."

"I haven't harassed you, have I? I've been try[ing to]
keep my distance." He thought about the last cou[ple of]
days. Samantha had seemed more relaxed. He'd [won-]
dered why. Was it because she was contemplat[ing a]
change in their relationship?

She shook her head and he stepped closer. Wrapping his hands around her arms, unsure whether he was stopping her from coming closer or ensuring she didn't run away, he said softly, "Honey, are you sure?"

She nodded again.

"Honey, you're going to have to speak to me before—before anything happens. I can't just—" He could, of course. His body was racing at even the thought of being with Sam. But he had to know for sure that this was what she wanted.

In a low voice, as she stared at his chest, she said, "Yes, I'm sure. When you kiss me, I—I want more, Rich. What we have is special, but I want more."

"So do I. Big time. You make me so hot I can barely control myself. These past few weeks have made life difficult for me. But I can wait if this is too fast for you. We can get to know each other better."

She placed her hands flat on his chest. "I didn't know I'd have to work this hard to convince you."

Rich swallowed hard. "Maybe we should, uh, start out kissing and see where it leads. I'll stop whenever you want me to."

He waited for her response, his heart beating double time. All he got was a slight nod, her gaze fixed on his lips. That was enough encouragement for him. He wrapped his arms around her, pressing her against him. A perfect fit.

"You're sure?" he asked again.

She sighed. Then she took his hand from her back and lay it across her left breast. "Can you feel it beating, Rich?"

"Oh, yeah, honey, I can feel it." His lips dipped to hers, and the rest of the world disappeared. They were lost in sensations. He slid his hand up her back, under her T-shirt, feeling her bare skin for the first time since he'd rubbed that muscle cream on her shoulder. But this time, miracle of miracles, he didn't have to hold back.

Her silken skin invited his touch and he was soon searching for the bottom of her T-shirt so he could lift it over her head. "I need to see you," he whispered as he forced his lips to leave hers long enough to tell her. She pulled his mouth back to hers, but she'd heard him. She helped him remove her shirt. Then her fingers began working on his shirt snaps with such effectiveness, she was pulling his shirt off in no time.

She didn't even seem to notice when her bra followed. Instead, she reached for his belt buckle. He knew he needed to get something on the hay before they could lie down. He was going to tell her, but his lips were drawn to hers again. He solved the difficulty, lifting her against him and carrying her to the tack room.

Inside, he grabbed a bedroll they kept there for nights he was up nursing a sick horse. He lay her down and joined her on the bedroll. "Sam—Sam, if you're gonna say no, it had better be soon," he warned her, his breath shallow. He waited in agony for what seemed like days before she answered.

"Love me, Rich. Please love me."

His lips took hers again and he helped her out of her jeans. She returned the favor. After checking to be sure she was ready, he entered her, unable to hold back any longer.

Until he reached a barrier.

Unable to stop himself, he plunged through, but his pleasure had disappeared. She was a virgin.

"Sam! Sam, I'm sorry!"

"What's wrong?" she asked, her breathing still shallow, her voice distracted.

Withdrawing now would serve no purpose. He started again to build the tension, the emotion, the need. Without answering her question, he led her to passion again. When he felt her release as she clutched him, holding on for dear life, he let go, too.

SAMANTHA LAY ON the bedroll, hardly aware of her nakedness. She'd just experienced the most incredible, emotional event ever. Slowly she became aware of her surroundings.

Beside her, Rich sat up. "Are you all right?"

She had known there would be pain, but the passion that followed easily overruled it. "I'm fine," she said, hearing the wonder in her voice. She hadn't known love with a man could be like that.

"Why didn't you tell me?" Rich said.

She turned to stare at him, hearing the anger but not understanding. "What?"

"That you were a virgin."

"Does it matter? Did I not do it right?"

"Hell! You did it too well. Once I realized—I tried to hold back, but I couldn't."

She shook her head, as if trying to clear it. "But I didn't want you to hold back."

"Yeah, well, I guess I didn't, either. I'm sorry, Sam,

I meant to take it easy, to give you plenty of time
you know, change your mind, but somehow you se
on fire, every time. I forget everything when yo
Damn! I forgot a condom. I always use a condom!

She stared at him but he couldn't read her mind.
it the right time of the month for you to— I mean,
possible that you—'' He stopped when her eyes
with tears. "Sam, don't cry."

"I—I bought some." She sat up and grabbed
jeans and pulled out a small box.

Rich scratched his head. He wasn't sure what
wanted him to do with the condoms now. "It's a
late, honey."

She didn't appear to see the humor in their situa
"But I bought them!" she insisted, big fat tears run
down her cheeks.

He cuddled her against him. "Sssh, honey, don't
Everything will be all right, I promise." Smoothing
hair back from her face, he rocked her against
trying to offer comfort. Until he realized his b
wasn't out for the count. And it was way too soo
suggest anything but comfort now.

He eased her back, noting the stricken look in
eyes. "Let's get dressed and go back to the house.
get a good night's sleep and we'll work everything
in the morning. Okay?" He kissed her swollen lips
ended the kiss quickly.

He'd try that again when they were both dres
Then maybe he could restrain himself.

Samantha tried to think clearly, but it wasn't e
Suddenly her nakedness embarrassed her. She rea

for her clothes. His attempt to help her resembled the Keystone Kops. "Please, get dressed," she begged. It wasn't easy to ignore his lean, muscled body. She couldn't believe she could want him again, when she'd made such a mess of everything.

He realized he might as well get dressed. He had a sinking feeling she would leave as soon as she was covered, as if she couldn't stand to be around him. He tried to reassure her again. "Everything will seem better—I mean, we'll talk in the morning. Everything will be all right."

He was pulling on a boot when she stalked to the barn door. "Wait, honey." He almost lost his balance in the process, but he got to the barn door thirty seconds after her. She didn't slow down or cut him any slack.

He caught her arm before she started into the house. "Sam, please wait. I want to tell you—what happened was—"

She filled in the blanks with words he hadn't had in mind. "A mistake!" Then she slammed the door behind her.

RICH STAYED OUT on the porch until his body had recovered from their lovemaking. He'd already realized sex with Sam would be great. Now he had absolute proof.

"Damn!" He suddenly remembered he hadn't asked her to promise not to run away. He'd done so each night this week. But he was being silly. She wouldn't be able to get away before he talked to her in the morning. He'd make everything right then.

He had to. He was beginning to realize that a life without Sam would be—nothing. Nothing at all. He relived those minutes in her arms, holding her close, loving her, and he decided he'd just gotten lucky. Not having sex. He didn't mean that. He meant that he thought he'd found the kind of love his parents had. At least *he* had. He was going to have to work on Samantha. But he would. He was a fighter. And Samantha was worth the fight.

His thoughts were spinning and he decided he should get some sleep as he'd advised Samantha. He'd need to be up early to catch her before his grandma wanted to know what was going on. But once he told her Sam was going to be his wife, he knew she'd be happy. He leaned against the porch rail, dreamily picturing her joy and his parents' faces when he told them. He wondered if Sam would want to continue living with his grandmother or build their own house. He'd let Sam make that decision.

Feeling pretty proud of himself for how things had turned out, even though he hadn't planned any of it, and deeply satisfied with the best sex he'd ever had, he went in the house with a smile on his lips.

It was still there when he went to sleep.

SAMANTHA WAS UP before dawn the next morning. It took only a few minutes to pack. She left all the things she'd acquired during her time on the ranch behind, except the money she'd been paid.

Knowing Lavinia and Rich would be up by six-thirty,

she was determined to take the car and leave at six. The bus left the store at seven.

She took the time to write a note of love to Lavinia. In the last line, she left a message to Rich, simply saying she couldn't do it. He would know what she meant. She couldn't write any more or she would start crying. Every time she thought about going away, tears pooled in her eyes. She tried not to think about last night at all.

She'd planned so carefully to ensure that her actions wouldn't hurt anyone. Then she'd forgotten the condoms. How could she? She hadn't realized the power of what she'd experienced. And wanted to experience again. She'd been so foolish, thinking she would take away a beautiful memory. Instead, she was taking away a load of guilt.

She loved Rich. She'd love to be a member of his family. But she wanted a marriage like Pete and Janie's, or any of the Randalls'. And that wasn't what was going to happen. And to know she'd risked the possibility that she was pregnant… ''Stupid, stupid, stupid,'' she whispered. But her hand cradled her stomach even as she said it. If she really was pregnant, she'd make a home for her baby. She'd cherish it, no matter what it took.

After tiptoeing down the stairs with her duffel bag, Sam made herself a peanut butter sandwich and grabbed a soda. It would have to last her a while. Then, she took the keys off the pegboard by the back door and stole out as the sky was just beginning to brighten.

She hated taking the car, but she would leave it in

town, giving the keys to the young lady who'd sold her the ticket, knowing she'd call Lavinia then.

Fifteen minutes later, she was standing on the sidewalk in front of the general store, waiting for the appearance of the big bus. There were only two other people waiting for the bus so far, and she didn't know either of them. She was home free—except for the pain of leaving.

RICH ROLLED OVER and opened his eyes, but he didn't get out of bed at once. Instead, he relived last night and the pleasure he'd experienced making love to Samantha. And soon, he'd wake up with her beside him each morning.

A satisfied smile filled his face. This marriage thing wasn't even scary when he pictured Samantha walking down the aisle to him. Funny how things worked out.

Maybe now he even understood his twin's choices. At first, he'd been upset that Russ had put Abby before him. They'd always been first with each other. So Rich had gone off to the rodeo. But now, he thought he owed Russ an apology. He finally understood about love.

Whoa! He loved Sam. He'd known it last night, but he hadn't actually thought those words. He loved Sam. And he loved what they'd done last night, but...he wanted to be sure. He tried to picture someone else by his side, but he couldn't. He tried picturing several sexy ladies in the role of his wife, and realized it was Sam, not anyone else, that he needed. How lucky could a guy get!

He loved Samantha Jeffers.

That thought didn't even faze him. He, Rich Randall, man-about-town, was in love. Had he told Sam that last night? No. He'd told her they would talk this morning. He'd told her it would be okay.

"Damn! It's a wonder she didn't find a gun and shoot me!" he exclaimed, shoving back the covers. He had to tell her. Now!

He pulled on his jeans and hurried to Sam's bedroom, deciding there could be an extra benefit to awakening her. He could kiss her, hold her.

He slipped into her room, only to discover the bed made. She was up early? He spun around, heading for the kitchen, when something about the room had him turning around again. He hurried to the closet.

It was gone. That damn duffel bag was gone. The one thing Sam would never leave without. She'd gone!

The phone rang as he headed downstairs, praying he was wrong. He grabbed it as he entered the kitchen. "Sam?"

"No, it's Doc. I just saw Sam standing on the sidewalk in front of Sarah and Jennifer Waggoner's general store. Looked to me like she's waiting for the bus!"

"Doc! Get over there and keep her from getting on it. I'll be right there!" he said urgently. He hung up while Doc was still talking, but all that mattered was Sam.

He ran up the stairs, awakening his grandmother with all the noise.

"Rich? Is that you? What's wrong?"

"Sam's gone!"

He grabbed a T-shirt and his boots. Then it occurred

to him that she might've taken his grandmother's car. His truck was still at his dad's. He looked out the window and confirmed his suspicion. He called his dad. "Sam's run away and I need my truck. Can you bring it over?"

"Be right there," his father agreed, asking no questions.

As he raced down the stairs again, he told Lavinia, "I'm going to get her."

Instead of waiting for his father, Rich began jogging down the driveway. He couldn't risk waiting. He needed Samantha in his life. He couldn't let her get away.

Rich was almost to the end of the driveway when he saw his black truck. Pete pulled over and reached out to open the passenger door. Rich jumped in. "Let's go!"

"What happened?" Pete growled as he floored the gas pedal.

Rich didn't know how to answer. "I don't know. Last night everything was—" He didn't want to go down that road. "This morning Doc called to say she's on the sidewalk waiting for the bus."

Pete looked at his watch. "I think the bus comes in at seven. We should be able to get there about five minutes before."

Rich nodded, his gaze fixed forward, as if he could will them to get to town faster.

"Are you wanting to marry her? I thought you said—"

"I've been an idiot."

"What happened?"

"I didn't know— I realized this morning I love her, but I haven't told her yet."

Pete said nothing, his jaw clenched.

"I said everything wrong. This morning, I jumped out of bed and hurried to her room to tell her the right things, and she'd gone."

"You'd better pray, son. You've just about blown your chance."

"I know."

SAMANTHA WATCHED AS Doc made a U-turn and pulled up in front of the general store. She tried to hide behind a pole. She didn't want anyone to see her.

"Mornin', Sam!" Doc sang out, causing the others waiting for the bus to stare at her.

"Um, mornin', Doc. What are you doing out this early?"

"Checking on one of my patients. How about you?"

Samantha had to come up with some excuse. "Um, I'm going to Casper to do some shopping."

"Ah. Why don't you just drive? There's Lavinia's car," he pointed out.

"She—she might need it during the day."

"Thoughtful of you," Doc said, but he looked over his shoulder down the road toward Lavinia's place.

Samantha looked that way, too, to see if the bus was coming.

"There it is," a kid called out. He'd already told Samantha he was going to visit his grandmother.

Sam's grip tightened on her duffel bag and she

stepped forward. Her heart was beating rapidly, even as it was ripping apart.

She stared at the bus, growing larger as it sped down the road. Just before it got to the city limits sign, a black pickup ripped around it. Before Sam could even move, it whipped to a stop in front of her, scattering a few pebbles out of the road.

"Sam!" Rich shouted, bounding out of the truck and onto the sidewalk. "What the hell do you think you're doing?"

Samantha closed her eyes, asking herself why he hadn't been ten minutes later. "I'm leaving. Please, just let me leave."

"You can't leave!" he exclaimed.

"There's no law against it," Sam assured him. "Here are the keys to Lavinia's car. I was going to leave them here, but you can take them."

He caught her by the shoulders and pulled her to him. She pushed him away. "Stop!"

"You okay, Sam?" Pete asked.

It hadn't occurred to Samantha to wonder who was driving Rich's pickup. "Pete? What are you doing here?"

"Rich needed his truck. And I wanted to know why you were leaving without saying goodbye."

Sam's eyes filled with tears. "I—I have to. Will you tell Janie—will you tell her goodbye for me?"

"You're not leaving!" Rich shouted.

"Yes, I am!" she shouted back. "You don't have the right to keep me here."

Even though it was early in the morning, they were

drawing a crowd. The bus pulled to a stop just behind
Rich's truck. The sheriff, too, parked by the store.

"Morning, everyone," the sheriff said. "Got a call
there was a problem here."

"No! No, but he won't let me leave," Sam said, her
voice rising in panic. "Tell him, Sheriff. Tell him I have
the right to leave."

"You sure do, little lady. I'm surprised he'd try to
stop you after seeing you take on that bully. Aren't you
afraid, Rich?"

"We're pulling out in five minutes," the driver
warned. "Everybody get on board."

Sam tried to move in that direction, but Rich was still
holding on to her. "Sam, I have to talk to you."

"No!"

"But we've got to talk!"

"No." She pushed her way past him and got on the
bus.

"Dad? Do you have any money on you? I forgot my
wallet."

Pete fished into his back pocket and pulled out some
bills.

"Don't let the bus leave!" Rich shouted and hurried
into the store to buy his own ticket.

"What's he doing?" Sam stuck her head out the window and shouted.

"It appears, he's going with you," Pete said with a
grin.

"He can't do that!"

"He has to if you won't let him explain. I reckon

even he can clear things up by the time you get to Denver.''

Samantha stared at Pete. The thought of having Rich beside her for eight hours was disturbing. ''Pete, I have to leave.''

''Honey, if you'll give him a chance to explain, then I'll make sure you get where you want to go, if he hasn't changed your mind.''

''But—you promise? I won't have to wait until the next bus?''

''Nope.''

Rich came out of the store, heading for the bus. He didn't even say anything to his father.

Samantha met him at the door on her way off the bus.

''Sam!'' he exclaimed, jerking her off the bus into his arms.

She loved being in his arms again, but she couldn't stay. ''I haven't changed my mind. But Pete said I could go anyway, if I'd just listen to you.''

Rich let her slide down his long body and stared at her. Abruptly, he said, ''Okay,'' took her hand and started walking.

''Wait!'' she protested. ''Not—not any place private!''

Rich looked frustrated, but Pete suggested they go to the café. ''You two can get a separate booth, and I'll buy Doc and the sheriff breakfast for disturbing their morning.''

"WHY DID YOU LEAVE? We said we'd talk this morning." Rich asked as soon as the waitress had given them cups of coffee.

Samantha kept her head down. "I know."

"Why? I thought we would—would be together."

She shook her head without looking up.

"Sam, what happened last night, it was going to happen sooner or later. We're—we're destined for each other!"

"You're saying that because you feel responsible. It's okay, Rich. I'm used to being alone."

He reached across the table and stroked her cheek. "But I'm not."

She looked up at him, surprised by his response. "That's ridiculous. You're not alone. You have lots and lots of family and friends."

"Yeah, I do, but it wouldn't matter if you leave. This happened faster than I thought, Sam, but I know I need you. I know without you, I'll always be alone." He stared at her, pleading with every ounce of his being.

"I don't— You're just saying that because it was my first time. But I asked you. You didn't— I had to plead for you to—" She broke off, her face red.

"Will the next time be your first time?" he asked softly.

She frowned. "Of course not."

"If I promise to ask you this time, will that take care of the problem? Honey, it wasn't that I didn't want to. But I thought it might be too soon for you. I wanted you, always, but I didn't want you to regret anything. And I sure as hell don't want you to run away."

"You said you didn't want to get married."

"I lied!" he assured her with a grin.

Tears pooled in her eyes and she shook her head helplessly. "I don't know what to say."

"Sweetheart, all I'm asking is that you give me some time. I'm ready to marry you right now, but if you want some time, to be sure, I'll wait. As long as you don't leave."

She looked away. "I'm thinking about you, Rich. I'm not right for you, for your family." He gave her an incredulous look and she hurried on, trying to explain. "It's not that I don't love you, but I have to do what's right."

Before she even finished speaking, Rich leaped to his feet and gave a cowboy yell. Then he caught her hands and pulled her up from the booth. Before she knew what was happening, he wrapped his arms around her and kissed her.

When he finally released his lips from hers, he whispered, "We'll get the license tomorrow."

Her head was spinning. "Didn't you hear me? I'm not right for you."

"Yes, you are," Rich assured her. "Sweetheart, I want to go to bed with you every night, and wake up beside you every morning. I want us to have lots of children, but I'll always want you first of all. We Randall men know how important our ladies are. You're my number one. I realized that last night but you were crying and— Why were you crying?"

"I planned everything. Then once you kissed me, I forgot the condom and risked having a baby," she said softly, hiding her face in his chest.

"Don't you want to have my baby?"

"Yes, but it would be irresponsible to do so when I'm on my own. The baby would suffer."

"But you're not on your own anymore. Do you hear me, Samantha? We're together, and we'll always be together, because we love each other. Will you come back home, and give me a chance to prove it to you?"

Her only response was a gentle nod, but her gaze was full of love, and once again he kissed her. Her arms slid around his neck and she met his hunger with her own.

"Are you gonna argue with me now, Rich Randall?" a voice intruded.

He lifted his head to see Mona, a big grin on her face, standing beside him. She looked at Sam. "I told you you'd better pick out that wedding gown, and I was right."

"Yes, you were," Sam shyly agreed.

Pete joined them. "Did you get things settled?"

"Oh, yeah," Rich said with deep satisfaction.

"Pete," Sam asked anxiously, "You won't mind if— if we marry?"

"If?" Rich protested. "If? You've already agreed, Sam, and I'm not about to let you out of our agreement."

"Besides," Mona added. "I already predicted it, and I'm never wrong."

"She's right," Rich replied. "We were meant for each other."

Samantha could only agree.

Epilogue

A knock on the door sent a flutter of activity through the room. "It's time," Tori announced, her voice breathless. "Are my flowers on straight?" She turned to the closet mirror to be sure the halo of flowers, vibrant against her pale hair, hadn't slipped.

"You look beautiful," Anna, her mother, assured her. "That blue looks good on all of you."

The young Randall ladies lined up at the door. The last two, Elizabeth and Tori, the maids of honor, checked the two ladies in white. "Ready?" they both asked.

Abby and Samantha nodded, their eyes sparkling with joy. Everything was perfect.

Samantha thought of the changes she'd experienced the last few months, and the remarkable family she would be a part of for the rest of her life. Russ and Abby, in particular, had asked them to share their wedding. So the brothers who'd lost each other because of love, had rediscovered their closeness through love. If Sam had had any doubt about Rich's feelings, they would've been dismissed when she overheard Rich apologizing to his twin.

"It wasn't that I wasn't happy for you, Russ. But I didn't understand how overwhelming love could be. Now, I do."

As the brothers embraced, Samantha treasured those words to her heart, to remember forever.

They stepped out into the foyer, Abby taking Jake's arm as he led her down the aisle. And then Pete offered his arm to Samantha, leaning to kiss her cheek and whisper, "Now, you really will be my daughter."

Samantha was thrilled that Pete's remark was true. But most important of all was the man waiting at the end of the aisle. Rich was going to be her husband.

Standing there, tall and proud in his tuxedo, he would impress anyone. But most impressive of all was what was inside. A caring, kind, loving man. And he wasn't ashamed to show it, a legacy from his father and uncles.

Samantha would never be alone again.

* * * * *

*Victoria's story will be coming in July
from Harlequin American Romance.
And next month, watch for
SUMMER SKIES,
a special two-in-one volume
from Harlequin Books
and Judy Christenberry,
containing the stories of two of
the original Randall brothers.*

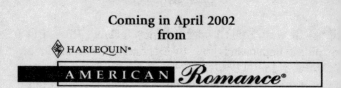

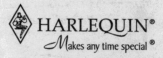

Every day is

A Mother's Day

in this heartwarming anthology
celebrating motherhood and romance!

Featuring the classic story "Nobody's Child" by Emilie Richards
He had come to a child's rescue, and now Officer Farrell Riley was
suddenly sharing parenthood with beautiful Gemma Hancock.
But would their ready-made family last forever?

Plus two brand-new romances:

"Baby on the Way" by Marie Ferrarella
Single and pregnant, Madeline Reed found the perfect husband in the
handsome cop who helped bring her infant son into the world. But did his
dutiful role in the surprise delivery make J. T. Walker a daddy?

"A Daddy for Her Daughters" by Elizabeth Bevarly
When confronted with spirited Naomi Carmichael and her brood of girls,
bachelor Sloan Sullivan realized he had a lot to learn about women!
Especially if he hoped to win this sexy single mom's heart....

Available this April from Silhouette Books!

Silhouette®
Where love comes alive™

TRUEBLOOD, TEXAS

Coming in May 2002...

RODEO DADDY
by

B.J. Daniels

Lost:

Her first and only love.
Chelsea Jensen discovers
ten years later that her father
had been to blame for
Jack Shane's disappearance
from her family's ranch.

Found:

A canceled check. Now Chelsea
knows why Jack left her. Had he ever loved her, or had she
been too young and too blind to see the truth?

**Chelsea is determined to track Jack down and find out.
And what a surprise she gets when she finds him!**

Finders Keepers: bringing families together

HINTBB